"Not that the story need be long, but it
will take a long while to make it short."
— Henry David Thoreau

The Day is Dark
and
Three Travellers

Born in 1939 in Quebec City, Marie-Claire Blais left school
at 15 to work in a shoe factory. The publication of her first
novel when she was just 20 attracted the attention of
Edmund Wilson and won her a Guggenheim Fellowship.
Her 1965 novel, *A Season in the Life of Emmanuel,* is perhaps
her best known work and was awarded the Prix France-
Canada and the Prix Medicis. *The Manuscripts of Pauline
Archange* and *Deaf to the City* have won Governor General's
Awards. Marie-Claire Blais now lives a reclusive life in
Montreal.

Janet M. Paterson teaches Québec Literature at Erindale
College, University of Toronto. She has written a book on
Anne Hébert and is currently preparing a study on
postmodernist fiction in Québec.

THE DAY IS DARK
and
THREE
TRAVELLERS

Marie-Claire Blais

with an Introduction
by Janet M. Paterson

Penguin Books

Penguin Books Canada Ltd., 2801 John Street, Markham, Ontario, Canada L3R 1B4
Penguin Books Ltd., Harmondsworth, Middlesex, England
Penguin Books, 40 West 23rd Street, New York, New York 10010 U.S.A.
Penguin Books Australia Ltd., Ringwood, Victoria, Australia
Penguin Books (N.Z.) Ltd., 182-190 Wairau Road, Auckland 10, New Zealand

First published in French in Canada under the titles *Le Jour est Noir*
and *Les Voyageurs Sacrés*

First published by Farrar, Straus and Giroux

Published in Penguin Books, 1985

Manufactured in Canada by Webcom Limited

Canadian Cataloguing in Publication Data

Blais, Marie-Claire, 1939-

(Le jour est noir, English)
The day is dark

(Penguin short fiction)

Translation of: Le jour est noir, and Les voyageurs sacrés.

First published: New York : Farrar, Straus and
Giroux, 1967.

ISBN 0-14-007911-4

I. Blais, Marie-Claire, 1939-   Les voyageurs
sacrés. English. II. Title. III. Title: Le
jour est noir. English. IV. Title: Three travellers.
V. Title: Les voyageurs sacrés. English. VI. Series.

PS8503.L35J6813 1985   C843'.54   C84-099647-0
PQ3919.2.B53J6813 1985

Contents

THE DAY IS DARK

and

THREE TRAVELLERS

INTRODUCTION
by Janet M. Paterson

Occasionally writers are the most perceptive critics of the works of other writers. When *The Day is Dark and Three Travellers* was first published in English, it received an insightful and favourable review by Robertson Davies in the *New York Times Book Review*. While stating that "the writing of this extraordinary young woman is so individual, so unlike anything else being written on this continent," Davies suggested that admirers of her poetic vision of life may find these novellas even more to their taste than her novels.

However, it is only when we look at the full career of this writer that we can fully understand the scope of her "extraordinary" quality. In her youth, Blais was certainly not groomed for a literary career. Born into a working-class family in 1939 in Quebec City, she was discouraged from writing by her parents who feared the economic sacrifices that would result from such a choice. In spite of an early interest in creative writing and literature, in 1956 Blais left school (a girl's convent) to work in various offices. Soon after, however, she moved away from home in order to be able to write in, what Virginia Woolf would have called "a room of her own."

With the publication of *La Belle Bête* in 1959, Blais's career was launched. She spent a year in Paris on a Canada Council Fellowship and, in 1963, she was awarded a Guggenheim Fellowship with the sponsorship of Edmund Wilson. Blais was now clearly being encouraged to write. And with such encouragement, her writing flourished; she published at an astonishing pace. In fact, as her friend Barbara Deming's comments reveal, Blais's life became her writing: "I have never known anyone who works more continuously. Even when she is not at her desk, actually writing, even when she is just sitting quietly with a friend, one can sense often that her thoughts are haunted still by the characters to whom she is giving life."

Having written, over a period of twenty-five years, more than fifteen novels (many of which have been translated into several languages), twenty-three plays, numerous poems and essays, Blais, who now lives in Montreal, candidly stated in an interview that writing for her constitutes an aesthetic and human adventure which she is determined to pursue to the end: "I want to go as far as possible."

Throughout this author's work, there are two elements that remain constant. First, there is a gloomy vision which pervades her entire fictive universe, a vision which uncovers with brooding intensity the dark side of our contemporary world. Images of death, poverty, sexual depravity and suffering recur constantly. The forces of evil are deemed to be so powerful that they can destroy not only love but life's primal force. Some readers may find – as indeed some have found – this vision excessively bleak and pessimistic, particularly because it frequently describes the world of adolescence. And yet, it is precisely this dark realism which confers power and originality to Blais's prose. For if this author has become a significant figure in Canada's literary landscape, it is largely due to her iconoclastic writing. She has portrayed oppressive forces, alienation, and despair with remarkable constancy and vigour.

There is also another factor which characterizes her prose. Astonishingly, in the midst of horrible images, we find a rare poetic quality. Blais's writing is lyrical and inventive; her style is original and compelling. Clearly, she is a writer who is intimately connected to her craft. Skillfully using "poetic" techniques, she experiments freely with stream of consciousness, with shifts in narrative voice and changes in time and space. For Blais, art represents a formal as well as an existential pursuit, a pursuit which is grounded on the firm belief in the importance of the writer in our society: "I believe that artists, thinkers, philosophers can change something because words are strong. That is all we have, words to show our revolt."

In the first novella reprinted here, *The Day is Dark,*

we are invited to enter a strange world, a dreamlike world enveloped by shadows and fog. On many levels, this story dramatizes the opposition implicit in the title, where darkness is contrasted to daylight, where life is opposed to death, love to betrayal, and hope to despair. Ostensibly, this story is about three young couples whose love is doomed because of their inability to accept reality or the values of the adult world. While there are numerous glimpses of love (especially sexual and maternal) in this strange world, ultimately it is a vision of despair which prevails. But what kind of despair? That of a generation defeated by lack of courage? A careful reading of the story reveals that the darkness is universal in its scope and historical in its dimensions:

> A night with no awakening takes shape before me: are we under sentence of death? Are we the shadowy generation chosen to witness the end of the world? Are my doubts simply the presentiment of an ineluctable horror?

In a world threatened by nuclear destruction, these words have a powerful resonance. But readers will notice that a glimpse of hope marks the end of the story. Joshua's return can be viewed as the triumph of daylight after darkness, a possible victory, in other words, over the title's bleak foreshadowing.

The second novella, *Three Travellers* has been considered by several critics to be one of Blais's most beautiful and lyrical pieces of prose. On the level of form, this is an unusual story: it is a ''prose poem'' which shifts readily from poetry to prose, from prose to poetry, frequently blending both genres. This style might be viewed as an exercise in pure aesthetics, were it not for the fact that the form is closely related to the meaning. Essentially, *Three Travellers* is a story about art, not about fleeting or profane art, but about art that is sacred and transcendental. Ultimately, it seeks to tell us about the profound relationship of life to art.

Here again, on the level of the plot, we have primarily a love story. A young sculptress, Montserrat, who is happily married to a playwright, Miguel, falls in love with a brilliant pianist, Johann. This love relationship becomes so intense and complex that the only possible outcome is death. Johann continues to live through his art and his newborn child, but the young couple, Montserrat and Miguel, must face a tragic death. A banal story? Undoubtedly, if it did not first and foremost speak about art. For it is surely not fortuitous that the three characters are artists, that the geographical places mentioned are important art centres (Paris, Vienna, Venice, Chartres), and that the narrative form is structured according to the movements of a concerto for piano (a concerto which is interpreted in the story by Johann). But if this story is about art, one may wonder why it ends with the juxtaposition of life and death – the death of the couple and the birth of Johann's child. Shortly before his death, Miguel says: "I have understood that infinite distance at last." Herein lies the meaning of the story. Art is sacred and transcendental; it is life, death, and redemption; it encompasses the past, present and future. In other words, art, even more than love, allows one to experience "that infinite distance."

THE DAY IS DARK

PROLOGUE

"And who's that over there?" Raphael asked.
"Joshua, that's Joshua," Marie-Christine said.

Marie-Christine looked at Raphael as he stood there with one foot in the shade of the cherry tree. She thought she liked him better than the summer before. He no longer had those cruel fists and those sulky lips. She also thought how bored she was with picking cherries.

Raphael crossed the sunlight in a single bound and ended up leaning into the patch of shade where Joshua stood watching Yance fill her apron with cherries and flowers.

"You're Joshua, I hear."

Joshua lifted his head to look at Raphael. Yance was gazing down into her apron as one kneels to look into a spring: she loved those gentle, lively colors in the warm wind. And Joshua was gazing at the little girl, silent beneath her long hair.

"They say you've just started at our school," Raphael said. "Where do you come from?"

"From the sea," Joshua said.

"I mean, where did you live, before you came here?"

"By the sea," Joshua said.

Joshua didn't feel at ease with his thirteen years. He was too tall, too somber. He was growing up with a startled grace that was not his own, like someone walking in his sleep. At last Yance looked up at him. Raphael laughed without knowing why, and the light rippled over his teeth; for a moment the boy's lips seemed wounded.

"It's nice here," he said.

Then Raphael ate some cherries and looked up into the sky. He was taller than usual as he stretched his neck so as not to look at his friends.

"Genevieve asked us to come in again at five," Yance told her brother.

"I'm too old to go in at five," Raphael said, cutting a shadow in two with his foot.

Raphael spat each of his cherry pits a long way away from him. Yance watched in admiration. It was something a man might do. Marie-Christine came over, and Raphael could see her knees and her bare feet.

"I'd like to go for a walk with you down to the stream," Raphael said.

Marie-Christine bent down and rubbed her right foot. "I can't. I've got a thorn in my heel."

"Ah! If you'd only wear shoes . . ."

"I like it when the grass caresses my feet like the rain."

"I'd like to go for a walk with you," Raphael said.

Yance was counting the cherries in Joshua's hand. "He's been picking green cherries."

Joshua came closer to Yance. "Is it true that there's only one stream running through the town?"

Raphael stretched himself, while the upper part of his face slowly broke into a smile. "Is it true that the sea is there where you come from?"

"Yes, of course, there are houses for the fishermen, and the sea, and fog."

"I'd like to see the fog," Yance said.

Joshua felt a slight pain inside himself as he talked about the sea. But there was no way of telling why. Marie-Christine was still rubbing her bare foot.

"I've got a thorn in my heel," she said.

"Be quiet," Raphael told her.

She immediately fell silent. And her silence was part of a gentle, childish docility that was nevertheless womanly too. Marie-Christine took pleasure in obeying Raphael's eyes.

"You'll be sick," Yance said.

Raphael raised his head and went on eating cherries and grimacing at the same time.

"It's Saturday today," he said. "You can do anything on Saturday."

Marie-Christine's face was a little pink with fever, or with the afternoon sun. "Raphael, carry me over to the tree. I want to sit in the hollow. My foot hurts too much to walk."

"That's not true," Raphael said.

Yance turned to Joshua. "Let's take the swings. They've chosen the tree."

They stood up on the swings and faced straight into the wind. Raphael was carrying Marie-Christine over to the tree.

"You're strong," Marie-Christine said.

She spoke right against the boy's face and he didn't dare look at her. The hollow in the tree was cozy, even prettier than a school bench. Marie-Christine pointed to a thick branch. "And there's a hollow there for you as well, but it's a bit rotten."

"The whole tree is rotten," Raphael said.

"Why is your voice strange like that when you talk about the tree?"

"I don't like rotten trees. They're like people who've died."

Now they were all together near the tree. Standing on their swings, Yance and Joshua could swing as high as Raphael's and Marie-Christine's feet. And the air flowing over their arms and through their hair was the same warm breath that cooled Raphael's and Marie-Christine's faces. Joshua swung higher and higher. Yance felt sad because she was no longer swinging with him in exactly the same rhythm: as he flew forward, she flew back, and she could no longer hear what he was saying. Joshua was breaking the equilibrium of the afternoon. You always felt there was a risk of some misunderstanding, of a quarrel, when you were with him.

Yance stopped her swing with an abrupt movement of her back and slid down to the seat. Then, pushing off with her feet, she began swinging again, unhurriedly, until she was moving to and fro in exact time with Joshua once more.

"Joshua is a boat," Raphael said.

"Joshua is a lighthouse," Marie-Christine said.

Joshua couldn't hear what they were saying. But he liked the feeling that there was someone down there below him; it reminded him of his father's house, when there was a gale battering at the window. On those nights, he would hear the women and the men of the house talking together in warm voices.

"When you say, 'My foot is bloody,' in a play, people listen."

"You're stupid," Raphael said.

"The sun is setting," Marie-Christine said.

She had grown older without being aware of it. There was a deliberate pathos in her voice. She was acting.

"Oh, be quiet," Raphael said. "You're never going to be an actress."

"Why not?"

"Because I don't want you to be."

She was silent at that. Then, in her sweet and candid voice, she said: "The sun is disappearing."

"Of course it is," Raphael answered.

"Joshua, what will you do when you're a man?"

They had stopped their swings. The day was coming to a close. Yance pressed her cheek against the rope of her swing.

"Tell me, Joshua, what will you do?"

"I shall have a house in the mist."

"Perhaps I'll come and visit you."

"Mist houses are too small."

"Then I'll make myself as thin as a shadow."

"Then you can come," Joshua said.

"Will you have any children?" Marie-Christine asked.

"No, I won't have children," Yance said.

Then she gave a solemn smile. "Perhaps one very little girl for Joshua."

"The house will have to be made bigger. It's dangerous because of the tides. Your little girl will die."

"She won't take up very much room. She can sleep against my shoulder. She can sleep in the palm of my hand. Like this . . ."

"Then that's all right," Joshua said.

Raphael dug into the bark of the tree with his teeth.

"You'll end up with fangs, like a wolf," Yance said.

Marie-Christine let herself slide back into the hollow of the tree. The leaves covered her so thickly that only her straw hat, her legs, and her arms could be seen. Her bare feet waved to and fro in the wind.

"I like it here," she said. "The leaves don't hurt me."

"I hate that rotten tree," Raphael said. "Don't wave your legs about like that," he ordered.

And she obeyed.

"And you, Raphael?"

"I'm a man now," Raphael said. "Today I do as I please."

"And what do you do?" Yance asked.

"I shall go to war and I shall die," Raphael said. "Perhaps I'll die very young, like my parents."

"Be quiet," Yance said.

She shook her shoulders like a rebellious child. Joshua admired her secretly.

"Our father killed himself last winter," Raphael said.

Marie-Christine emerged from her mossy hollow. Her hair shone in the light.

"What did you say, Raphael? I couldn't hear you."

"Nothing," Raphael said.

Joshua seized the rope of his swing in his fingers and pressed it against his chest. He was paying no attention to what Raphael was saying. Yance was swinging again, so fast that Joshua couldn't catch the outline of her legs and her skirt as she moved. She was like the wind.

She wasn't smiling any more.

"Why is she crying?"

They all remained silent. Marie-Christine jumped down from the tree.

"Let's go for a walk down to the stream," she said.

Joshua got up.

"Yance, are you coming?"

As she stepped down and stood beside him, Joshua looked for the tears on her face. He realized that the wind had burned them away.

"You'll never be able to keep up with me. Not with that thorn in your foot."

"I'll walk in front of you," Marie-Christine replied. "It doesn't hurt."

Raphael observed her out of the corner of his eye as she walked beside him. There was severity in his gaze, and his features had their usual air of fatigue and disdain.

"You look like a boy in those velvet pants," he said.

"We'll get there before them if we take the little path," Marie-Christine said.

"But the blouse suits you," Raphael added.

They were still a long way from the stream.

"Do you know how my father killed himself?" Raphael said.

Marie-Christine pulled her hat down over her eyes. Like that, swollen by the shadows, her lips had a greedy look.

"How hot it is!" she said.

"Do you know, Marie-Christine?"

"How hot it is!"

"Marie-Christine . . ."

"And yet it's a little bit cold too, somehow."

She was skipping as she walked. Her straw hat danced lightly like a hood.

"Was it true, about the thorn?"

"No."

"Then you tell lies?"

"Yes."

"Put your shoes on," Raphael said. "There are brambles."

"I'm not afraid of brambles."

Raphael looked at Marie-Christine's hands. They were fluttering and fragile, like the hands of little rich girls. Delicate and stupid. He disliked stupid hands.

"Are you going to become stupid later on, like all the other rich girls?" Raphael said.

"It's so nice to be rich," she said in tender tones, like a woman.

"I don't want you ever to be pretty," Raphael said.

"I don't either," she said.

Raphael's words scarcely brushed her awareness; she remained frivolous and impenetrable beneath her straw hat. And she did not want to get any older. It was late now.

They could feel it right inside. Marie-Christine was hiding herself away behind the feminine frivolity which consists of wanting to forget.

"I'm bored," Raphael said.

She crossed her arms. The smell of sun spread out all around her. That's how it always is. That was why Raphael was bored. He moved closer to her and took her neck between his fingers. As she amazed him with a slow, timorous gaze, he felt that this was what it meant to become a man.

"I want to go back now," she said.

And the more he pressed her neck, the closer to his lips he drew her face, all her face, the more he became aware of a painful unease being stirred up inside him by the sun. He kissed her on the lips. She stared into his eyes without comprehension.

"Don't you know yet?" he asked.

Marie-Christine lowered her eyes. Nothing was real yet. She wasn't going to be a young woman. (Everything was so nice before.)

"Let's go back."

"No," Raphael said. "It's too late to go back."

He was uncertain and proud. Dazed by her own feelings, Marie-Christine did not understand.

Raphael pressed her against him in silence.

"They've gotten lost," Yance said.

Yance shrugged her shoulders so that she could feel herself equal to Joshua, as subtle as Joshua. And as she raised herself to her companion's level, so she raised herself also to the level of the weakness that was there in Joshua's heart. The weakness of a dream. The shadows were all gone, and the sun was a long way off. A soft wind announced the rain.

"There's a storm coming," Joshua said.

He looked so tall and strong, but he was trembling like a little child.

"It's raining," Yance said.

He looked down at the stream and shivered with cold. Who is Joshua?

A curious animal . . . No, she wasn't able to say yet, not exactly, where this boy's soul had come from.

"What do you do when you go home?"

"My sister combs my hair and hurts my temples. I don't like going home."

"Let's wait for the fog," Joshua said.

He took Yance's hand between his fingers. But this was an unconscious gesture on his part. He was unaware of Yance's hand.

"Walk with me," Joshua said.

She drew away her hand. Joshua moved off alone into the fog. He took off his shoes and ran down to the bank of the stream. As he stood there, the sand turned into mud and blackened his ankles.

"I'm going back," Yance said.

But Raphael and Marie-Christine appeared at that moment, running toward her.

Raphael opened his mouth and stood drinking the rain.

"You've made Marie-Christine cry," Yance said.

Marie-Christine wiped her eyes with her wrist. "I'm all right."

Raphael was looking at the clouds.

"It's nothing. Only a thorn," Marie-Christine said.

And she wept, unashamedly. She wept with sudden sobs alternating with equally sudden silences: she wondered why she was crying so much. Then, quite shamelessly, she began again, unleashing a terrible childish willfulness, that boundless tide of grief which cannot belong to an untouched body or a virgin soul.

"Where is Joshua?" Raphael demanded.

"In the fog," Yance said.

Raphael turned his back on the two little girls and lit a cigarette. When he raised his head again, his face was wearing a mask of new and startling features.

"Be quiet," he said to Marie-Christine.

Little by little she fell silent, and stood gazing at Raphael from beneath lowered eyelids, like a cat. She had no idea that she was feeling a profound pity for him. The violence was there, pressing against her heart, but she wasn't ready for it yet. She was rejecting the new person she had now become against her own wishes; she was driving Raphael out from the untamed, instinctive world inside her.

Joshua reappeared out of the mist: a youthful stranger. Raphael took hold of Marie-Christine's wrist. Everything was accomplished.

She would remember always the monstrous solemnity that had just pressed down upon her. She had a feeling of being stretched out and out, of being made vulnerable to the whole world.

"Are you cold?" Raphael asked.

She bit her lips and said nothing.

"Perhaps you're too hot," Raphael said.

He let go of her wrist and began walking away.

"I'm going back," he said.

He moved away. Marie-Christine felt that she had yielded up her whole life during that transparent day. She was a living cry, and her solitude lay now like a weight on her belly and her breasts. Yet even her solitude was unknown to her. Yance looked at Joshua. He had preferred the fog to her words. He had preferred the stream to her friendship, yet Yance felt the need to protect him . . .

Two little girls stood disappointed, in the dusk. Illusions fall like dead leaves to the ground.

☆ ☆

"Now be good," Genevieve said. "I'm putting Nicolas to sleep."

"I didn't come home at five o'clock today," Raphael said.

Genevieve went on rocking the child. Raphael stared at the woman and the child. With pain at first, then with surprise.

"Sing," he said.

And Genevieve did as he asked.

The wind is heavy tonight, my Lamb,
And as I dreamed I lost my way,
Close your eyes tonight, my Lamb . . .

Raphael had forgotten how one puts a child to sleep. And Yance was once more experiencing the warmth that had overshadowed and comforted her heart, at five o'clock, as she sat in the swing. A fleeting sense of security like the presence of a fever inside a body that is too much alone: the pervading warmth of life.

She listened to Genevieve's voice and wondered at the tranquillity of her face. All her dizziness had disappeared as she sat by Raphael, in the big armchair. And since five o'clock Raphael had been a man. With this man in the house she would be like all the other sunlit little girls who forget the loneliness of their mornings and their nights. Genevieve put the child into its bed and turned out the lamp. The silence made its way slowly into the room; silence and the smell of silence . . .

Genevieve stroked their two necks with an unthinking hand, scattering tenderness with her absentminded austerity. Raphael shivered. He had stroked Christine's neck that afternoon.

"I shall be expelled from school," he said.

But as soon as he had said it, he left his sisters and went down to his own room.

Yance allowed her sister to comb her hair while she forced herself to decide in her own mind exactly why she had changed so much since the afternoon. There had been Joshua. There was nothing so very melancholy, after all, about a swing that won't swing quite as fast as the one beside it.

"And what were the cherries like?"

"Beautiful."

"And the sun?"

"Cold. Oh! You're hurting me. I'm going to have all my hair cut off."

She presented her blue-veined temples and her mist-damped hair to the stiff brush. Genevieve's fingers, accustomed to dealing with this chaos, flattened the recalcitrant locks with swift, crushing, downward strokes.

"Marie-Christine isn't Marie-Christine any more," Yance said.

"And the stream?"

Yance's tomorrow face was already there in her today face.

The street stretched ahead. It was as though there were no end to it, like the sky.

"I knew it all along," Raphael said.

"But you'd just begun to be sensible."

"They don't want me here any more," Raphael said.

He was sending the pebbles flying before him with the toes of his shoes. He was smoking as he walked along and eyeing the clusters of young girls as they came out of their private schools.

"I was bored there. It's a rotten school. I want to get away."

Then he lowered his eyes and stared at his young sister's feet as they walked along.

"Marie-Christine hasn't been at school at all since last Saturday," Yance said.

"Perhaps she's ill," Raphael said.

Yance closed her eyes.

"Oh, come on! You're not going to cry just because I'm leaving," Raphael said.

And he walked on, straight and solitary, and his step was wide and heavy . . .

PART ONE

*"It's no game," he said, "I was born like that, in
little pieces, motes of dust. To see me, you
would need an eye with multiple facets like
a fly, and all my generation is just like me."*

Bernanos, *Un Mauvais Rêve*

This evening I feel it's a marvelous thing to be a woman.
I am thinking about Joshua with a new heart: I have hope
in him.

Joshua is sitting thoughtfully by the fire. As I look at
him, I think how he revealed himself to me in a moment of
gentle languor, and how, even though we are bound together, we are still both free. He is twenty and I am
seventeen. He has been my lover for six months and I was
never able to feel this fascination before: he has become my
body's and my senses' brother with timid and yielding
tenderness, just as he has become my brother in spirit.

Yet through this sometimes distant sense of brotherhood we have still both kept our solitude and our separate dreams. Suddenly I feel a mysterious force urging me closer to him. Soon we shall be loving one another too much to be still free.

He is working at his dissertation. This is how I see him every day, at college, bent over his books, but I have never noticed that pulsing vein on his forehead before, or how his cheeks turn a little pink when he thinks really hard. There is a calm anxiety veiling his features and darkening his gaze: often now he is nothing more to me than the suffering on a face that is perpetually seeking to shut itself off from the world.

"Joshua . . ."

But the moment he lifts his head and gives me that pitiful look of his I know so well, I become aware of the silent laceration that is threatening him. Why did God create beings as close and as far away as Joshua? Men, far away in love and close in their suffering. They have no age, no times in which to live: everywhere, and with everyone, they are in exile. I am responsible for Joshua; he has been wounded by strangers, and there are other strangers who will wound him in the future; my heart fails me when I think that he might suffer with me too. I feel that he has been disappointed in other love affairs. An occasional word of disillusion tells me as much. That is all. He does not want to hide his life from me, but perhaps, out of some naïve modesty, he harbors a despairing affection for all those who have hurt him. He is sure of me. I am never certain of him: a quick-winged stranger, he might always leave me and then come back. He knows that I have made him my life's goal. Joshua has no goal at all himself, or rather, there is no goal he does not have. He attaches himself immoderately to people and to memories, and his dangerous capacity for scattering his emotions in any and every direction fills me with amazement. He believes it is his duty to love everything that is, and he is certain that God has rejected him. It pains me to see him surround himself with such clouds of fantasy and remorse. And tonight I bear the weight of him. "Oh! become supple and full of light, I shall be tired . . . tomorrow."

I stroke his forehead with the tips of my fingers. "You're feverish . . ."

I kiss his hair. He is motionless against my legs and I feel an ethereal desire for his whole being. Better not tell him about it. It is too simple a truth. I have always been aware of our desire I think, his and mine, but until this moment I had never experienced this extreme of tenderness that flowers in the inmost center of desire.

It will be late at night before Joshua begins to talk about going home. But I shall want to keep him here. Tomorrow our complicity will be locked away inside us. I shall be no more than a classmate. There must always be something left unspoken and unthought. He is going. I say nothing. My desire is too gentle. I stay standing here in the empty room, not daring to feel, my arms stretched out as though to crush the future against my breast.

I can still hear my sister's silvery voice. She is singing, to lull Nicolas to sleep or to sooth her own pain. Every night this pale supplication makes its melancholy ascent up to my room and awakens a mute rebellion in my heart. After our father's death, Genevieve divided the house between all the members of the family. I was thirteen then, Louis and Raphael were emerging from adolescence. We all inherited little self-contained apartments in the big house. Louis and Raphael were given the second-floor rooms; I had the whole of the first floor and total liberty. Later on, Louis and Raphael left the house. Genevieve shut up their rooms, with that gentle, backward-looking kind of loyalty that never resigns itself to deaths or absences.

She never stopped waiting for the two boys who would never come back. They had made new lives for themselves. Genevieve had brought my brothers up, and they had scarcely ceased to be children when they left her. She made no complaints. She had too great a need to believe in other people's liberty. And then, then there was Nicolas's illness . . .

And that too was a difficult leave-taking, a journey begun afresh each moment through a region of useless hope, since the child's life could not be saved. Genevieve refuses to face his approaching death. She still listens for the little boy running up and down the stairs and thinks: "I am going to make him better, I am going to save him." In a little while I shall see her leaning over my brother, frozen motionless in her own tears, and she will say: "Look, he's getting better already!"

Genevieve will always return to face that silence and the sick child.

And how could I escape from her despair?

Genevieve is losing her own being in Nicolas's slow death. She is taking leave of her own life without wishing it. Yesterday I still existed for her, my presence was indispensable; she avoided my confidences while nodding approval to some fragile enthusiasm that charmed or reassured her. Her affection was awkwardly expressed, a little abrupt, but sensitive; she was fiercely maternal in her attitude to Nicolas while deliberately avoiding such feelings toward me.

And now she is no longer alive. She has withdrawn into a laborious melancholy that resembles the arrogance of the defeated. Has Genevieve ever had lovers? Does she remember having been happy in their arms?

It is not within a human being's power to save a brother from death. He can only love him. Genevieve rejects this terrifying reality, just as she runs away from so many other realities. Tomorrow there will be Joshua but there will also be Genevieve. In her company I shall suffer the pain of her lie, which has lasted now for too long, and I shall shout at her: "That child is going to die." She won't listen to me. She will sing:

I love the wind when it rocks my child,
I love the night when it rocks the wind.

(And then, Genevieve, will you become aware of my presence, and will you give me a smile that will wipe out all trace of what was once Nicolas on your face? Your insane hope, your hope as predatory as grief itself, exploding there in your eyes . . .)

Toy trains and music boxes, all will soon be dead. All his playthings are sinking into silence. And I don't want to think of anything but my own life, as round and full as a fresh new season between my fingers.

☼ ☼

And what does death's corruption matter to me, since my love is in bloom? It is flowering in the warm sand of my veins. Joshua can gauge how fragile my gladness is.

September. October.

I am becoming a little more selfish now, so that I can appreciate Joshua's soul more clearly. We are two live and fervent bodies in the midst of a groaning humanity; we are two souls confronting the same fears; for his sickness, like mine, is youth. It is delicious to be understood in a single gaze, adapted to another body and to another set of troubled senses. And yet a child can never belong to another child. Joshua is not wholly mine, and it is good that it should be so. I know that he is turned to stone by the spells woven in my dreams, and that his attention is all directed to his own inner anguish. He belongs to himself more than to me.

I no longer want to see Genevieve. I am resigning myself to my love. I would like to forget the little tortured boy for whom I hear those songs at midnight . . .

And the wind has rocked the child among the stars

Joshua welcomes me into his house. In the silence of our nights, once restored to ourselves, we feel ourselves made richer yet also poorer without quite knowing why. I am in constant flight from a climate of disease. I excuse myself on account of my love and on account of my youth, but I am never convinced of being in the right. I haven't enough courage for the truth. I don't want to break the blackened crystal of my dream.

I sit through my lectures with a wandering mind. Joshua is serious about his work. But his fits of working are as feverish as his fits of boredom. We are truly close only in the evenings. Our eyes change. Our hands tremble. Perhaps it is our awareness of a second life in love that hurls us into some dizzying and luminous abyss. For Joshua, both order and disorder are attractive: he is never too tired to pursue his follies to the very end. He wants to climb every peak before he has even begun to live.

October. And already we are wiser. One night, at Joshua's, I pulled myself abruptly free of his embrace and said I had to go home.

"Nicolas has had an attack."

"Yance, you're just having a bad dream. You must get that little brother of yours out of your head. You ought to be living here with me."

How right he was! His gentleness cast a spell on me. I wanted nothing more than to give way to him. Next day Genevieve told me that Nicolas had been very sick during the night. By then he was calmer again and was playing in his bed.

"It's such a long time since he played!"

Genevieve was weeping with joy. I kissed Nicolas. Perhaps—or was I wrong to think it?—a miracle of will power performed in Genevieve's heart was capable of creating the illusion of health in his ravaged body.

"I've bought him a suit. He'll be better by Christmas."

I recalled Raphael as he said: "Sometimes hope is a terrible evil."

Deep inside me I can still hear Genevieve's worried voice and see her wasted face. "Then they came to the country of the ogres. When even the youngest of them stretched himself, the mountains would tumble down into the sea, and the stars went rushing through his hair."

I said nothing. I still haven't said anything.

The child is dead. I am not as astonished as I should be in the face of death. I can look at him without trembling. Just a little ten-year-old boy wrapped in eternal absence. Death is a series of faces to me: that was how I saw my father and mother on the threshold of my childhood. What weighed on me was Nicolas's life. My mind is exhausted and cowardly, I can feel that. I think of myself as hardhearted, standing stiffly here in front of my sister as she clutches the child to her. I'm not going to put my hand on her shoulder. There's no way of helping Genevieve. Joshua. My future is named Joshua. Tragedy in that face, too.

"I couldn't save him!"

Genevieve! But there's nothing I can say. She has grown old in these past few hours.

Is she twenty-five, or as old as fear? How her despair knifes into my flesh! The kind of despair that swells up in your chest like an icy need to vomit. And what if there is nothing in front of me at all? What if my mind is really half asleep?

"Genevieve, I won't leave you!"

I can't replace Nicolas. What is the use of such words? He was her child, her future, her present. She has prayed to the void to let her hear the child running happily through the house again, and there—look!—she is closing her eyes and moaning to herself. Couldn't I go away, like Louis and Raphael? I have loathed the savor of death that rules in this house, I have hated it so much, away from Genevieve as well as with her.

I am a young woman.

"Genevieve, I'm a woman."

She has forgotten me. But I will love and I will live. Leaving Genevieve means knowingly killing the little spark of life that still flickers inside her. I can't abandon her. I can't abandon myself.

"I couldn't save him."

And I seem to be hearing the melody that came through the walls to shatter my unquiet conscience:

And the child woke up on the moon,
The child who had wept on earth.

November. And still I am lying pale with anguish in Joshua's arms. I tried to forget about death. But it is stronger than all the youth in the world. Genevieve still sings at night. She no longer busies herself in my brothers' rooms in anticipation of their return or sits writing long, painful letters; the flesh is being eaten from her bones by a sterile passion. Without any doubt there exists a madness of hope, a madness that can make you contract your memory and your heart until there is no room to think of anything but Nicolas. Soon my sister will take up no room at all in the big house. She will be nothing but a cry.

Raphael has come back. Genevieve doesn't seem to recognize him. Without being jealous of my brothers, I know that Genevieve loved them more than she did me. Raphael has come back to a house of strangers, and he too talks to us about a world that is foreign to us. All I know of him is the secret wound that he has been trying to forget away from us: a first love and its failure. His adolescence is a thing of the past, but the wound is still alive. Raphael has forgotten nothing. And it will always be like this for him: leave-takings, ecstasies, and then this sad journey back to the impossible. What is it he has come back to relive here? Genevieve and I were so alone already!

"You're looking at me as though my face had grown hard."

"But it has grown hard, Raphael."

And he wanders around in his room and things no longer obey him as they used to. As a little boy, he was the master of his enchanted world: now he is the master of his solitude.

Things no longer obey him, because he has a man's hands. He left this house plunged in obscure suffering, and now he has been drawn back to it again.

"Do you think I haven't forgotten?"

He doesn't talk about the child. We are accomplices in a shared rejection of that death.

"You didn't want to forget," I said.

"How could I forget a disaster?"

He will still go on loving. He will go on loving always, but his love will be pitted against the desire for forgetfulness. (Raphael, Raphael, the disaster is what you carry inside you. It is as though your spirit yearns for the end of the world. You had no choice but to destroy your first love.)

I think of him. He thinks of me. And we do not recognize each other yet.

"Listen, we've got to bring this dying house back to life! And I'm going to have lots of friends! You are too, aren't you? Yance, do you hear what I say?"

Raphael thirsts after explosions and anger. Joshua is taken in by his gentleness. I am suddenly afraid of these two. From now on, our three lives will be obscurely mingled with each other.

"We're going to fight back against Genevieve, you by loving Joshua and I . . ."

"And you?"

"I've come home to win back Marie-Christine."

(Raphael, Raphael, remember how it was when you were only fifteen, when you wanted to love. And you thought that young girls would allow themselves to be crushed like playthings.)

"If you still love her, then you must love her in a new way."

He isn't listening to me. Is he dreaming about the little girl he initiated into love and into the penalties of love, one day when he thought he had become a man? And about the same little girl when she became a young woman, when she brutally left him, saying that she had been robbed of her childhood?

He is hiding his weariness by closing his eyes.

"I have come back to rest," he said. "Yes, I shall find rest with her."

"Joshua, I'd like to be married. I want to have a child."

It is Joshua's head pressed against my breast that makes me think of having a child. That dark head, how I have loved it in the mute voracity of our nights. That calm and comforting head. It has never hurt my flat belly. It has rested itself against my body; a friendly shape. At sixteen, when Joshua took me, I had a skimpy body that he set free from its hesitant night to awaken a woman's body that still remembers the virile hands from which it emerged more beautiful, and still trembling. In Joshua I had a companion in discovery, the father of my first womanly anxieties, and now a lover revealed, and in that lover a son. Does this man, this dreamer whom I have perhaps encouraged too much in his dreaming, does he have any presentiment, as I do, that we are setting our lives in the wrong direction?

He is calm, stretched out over my heart, rocked by an unknown force.

Married now, our life still obeys the rhythm of our blood. On certain evenings, Joshua doesn't come home to me but stays on alone in his old room. He has his free hours, just as he has a house and another life apart from me.

I am almost jealous of that novel he writes in the evenings beside the fire, torment in his face, and in those eyes, the disillusioned gaze of a man dead to everything but his own quest. He reads me poems written for me, the shadows of his soul, tender gusts from his inward storm. Joshua is learning how to be independent of me in all the things he does. But I, all I want is to be closer to him still.

Genevieve has given up the fight. Tall, untouched, she is an exile within her own hope and does not even leave her house any more. Like Raphael, she has built her own motionless paradise. I go up to make her dinners for her and reproach her for not wanting to live; I talk to her about the life and the movement that still go on outside, despite her grief. But she seems to have disappeared from the world. Then I tell her again: "Nicolas is dead." And she gives a strange smile.

Just before Christmas, she caught me burning Nicolas's things, his toys, his last pair of little new shoes. She followed my every gesture with a terrifying concentration, but she did not weep. Then she sang:

I love the wind when it rocks my child,
I love my angel's gentle eyes.

And I thought: "She is beaten. She has accepted."

I invited her to go out with me. I did her pretty hair for her. But I soon realized that she would only go back to her old, worn-out apartment. Already she had become a creature unable to love the sun. So then I drew the curtains, and the slow smell of time gone by burned into my senses.

That same evening, Genevieve changed to a new, more austere way of doing her hair. The small, hard bun surmounting her skull pulled at her temples and exposed the large expanse of her naked forehead. She was wearing a black dress with white cuffs. Relinquishing her role as a woman inconsolable in grief, Genevieve was visibly taking refuge in that of a woman keeping watch over the dead.

I can't count on Raphael to visit Genevieve. The sickness of the house attracts him, but my sister's sickness bores him. As though in defiance of his own hopes, out of stubborn pride, Raphael is perverting young girls. Can it be that I have seen in my brother's eyes the ironic flame of corruption? The soul of this house and my brother's soul too are decomposing between my fingers. And I can't feel anything to be so appalling that I must judge it. I hold my tongue. Visited by evil, I remain somber and empty, bound to other beings by passive ties of brotherhood.

There is Joshua's innocence, but even that is no longer perfect innocence, for it is able to cause pain to others. I no longer know which is right: good or evil, for both have a longing for eternity, a regret when faced with men's limitations.

I am expecting a child. Joshua stays home from college and enfolds me in an exquisite tenderness. He who has always been so silent is now always talking to me about the blind life that is growing inside me, like a rising flood. My head resting on his naked chest, I listen to him, fascinated by his eyes and lips.

"You see," he says, "we have life inside us and the whole world is waiting for it . . ."

With the knowledge of this incomparable wealth alive inside me, I feel myself to be older than Joshua, refreshed and already a mother. I kiss his hair, then his eyelids, inspired by a desire to console in him the future child still buried in the warm snows of my body.

Genevieve no longer vibrates in sympathy with my joy.

She has conjured away all the dust from her rooms. The furniture is so clean it glitters. She has shut up Nicolas's room at last. But she has not ceased her vigil. This new cleanliness is a mask for the chaos in her soul.

"I am expecting a child!"

And I expected at least a cry from that stone body. Nothing. She has even forgotten the words of her despair.

I am alone and pregnant. But I feel I have all the forces of the world at my beck and call. I am becoming more passionate, firmer certainly, direct and incisive, and fanatical. I blame Joshua for dreaming; I blame him for that sweetness of his, because I am afraid of being sated by it. I only want complete and certain things. Can't a man like Joshua give them to me then? I long for a balance in my life as one longs for fire to cauterize a bodily shame.

Ah! If only Joshua were mine, if only I knew his thoughts! But he can only assume whatever shape I give him. And he doesn't live inside the same flesh as I do.

"Couldn't we go away, Joshua? Why don't you take me to some other town?"

I don't dare tell him that it is some small part of himself that I am trying to forget in those other towns warm with spring, yes, that I am annihilating myself with him in the bustling impersonality of the crowds there, listening to the foolish and too human throbbing of their lives. And he allows me these brief trips in the same way as he covers my body with a sleepwalker's kisses, at night. As though he were humoring a sick child.

The long shadow of his face suddenly, and for the first time, makes me feel despairing. This is the way I could begin to loathe the way he looks.

I feel I am lost beside a boy even more lost than myself, though when I am surrounded by other people these misfortunes are neutralized. I have a husband on my arm, a child inside me, and I follow people in the street who follow me too because they no longer know what to do. My child will not grow up in a house of the dead, as I did. My child will be free. He will be Joshua but he won't be me. He is scarcely formed, I cannot hear him living yet: I am like that skinny adolescent Yance waiting for her breasts to fill out, or else for that cold and certain presence that would say: "I am here." As on my fourteenth birthday, I long to taste the harsh felicity of things already happening yet still incomplete.

Inwardly, I pity myself.

"Yance, do you want to go home?"

I can hear Joshua's voice. But I am still afraid of him.

"Are you with me or behind me, Joshua?"

He puts his arm around my waist. "We're together," he says.

Despite myself, I learn how to be simple during these trips; I laugh, I sing. I am a woman just like other women, delighted at being able to buy her husband a sweater, smiling into the mirror at Joshua so elegant in his corduroy jacket. And in the cafés where we waste so much time, doesn't it make me happy to drink out of the same glass as Joshua, as we used to do before, between lectures, foreheads pressed together over the table? It isn't possible to readapt oneself to student life when one is preparing to be a mother. Yet I should like to go back again to those careless truant days nevertheless and feel the old ecstasy at five o'clock as I watched the other students bursting out of their classes and clustering in the streets.

We have put our trips aside and taken up our old voracious satchels once again. Joshua prefers his studies to the solitude of my flesh. I huddle down beside the fire and dream. At Genevieve's, never a light-colored dress to be seen, or the bright cloud of her hair. She has become a woman meditating and reading the Bible in lethargic silence. She is forever giving birth to Nicolas in spirit: I am giving birth in my body, which is altogether ignorant of the lacerations in store for it.

And I am giving birth for Joshua, who is entirely ignorant of me. While my blood inside me seeks the obscure warmth of my dark breasts, Joshua sits writing at my feet. He writes, thinks, reads, and nothing changes for him. I cannot take Joshua's head onto my knees and stroke it there. I don't recognize it.

Joshua hasn't been home for several days. Tonight, worn out by my own inertia, I decided to go for a long walk, to walk aimlessly along the empty streets as though in quest of some inner hardening process to restore my sense of fulfillment. I remembered having taken such walks when I was fifteen. The footsteps and the cold. The penetrating cold that freezes your thoughts inside your head.

How long it had been since I had known a night of freedom! The fresh air sang in the hollow of my veins, on my cheeks, in my hair. I was seized by the strange drunkenness of springtime. I imagined that I was full of joy, but I was trembling with fright. Then, suddenly, I felt the baby inside me move for the first time, and that irresistible force alive in my entrails flooded me with pleasure. We were two lights shining in a loathsome night. For a moment I believed in God, in an all-powerful force of life inseparable from man's despair and hope alike!

And in the giants' hair
Stars fall . . .

The isolation of my body had given me the disproportion of a soul in prayer. And I who had never sought after God was sensing his presence, was loving him. At a time of love, bending down toward my heart, I had heard Joshua say to me: "With you in my arms I always believe we are bound for eternity. But it is only an illusion." I had seen his wandering gaze as it waited for some gesture capable of satisfying his hunger. And I had cried: "Joshua, my poor love!"

Where is it now, that spurting tenderness unaware even of itself?

The cold had frozen my shivering flesh into a marble

casing around my slowly beating heart. I passed a young girl running along with her scarf in her hand, and I longed to be able to run myself. The street lamps looked like pillars of warm mist. Rivulets of snow and water were vanishing over the edges of the sidewalks. I walked on as far as the park.

(The park is light at three o'clock in the morning.)

I watched the occasional couples escaping into the night. I felt a little unwell. I saw a silhouette that looked like my husband, with a young woman by his side. They were under the trees, talking, looking at one another, standing in silence. But it wasn't Joshua. It was a dream. The park wasn't a good place to be. There was too much wind. I decided to go back. The woman turned and pulled off her hat with one long, pale hand. I thought I saw Genevieve. But I was dreaming, again. Genevieve was in her room. I could see her lamp alight and the swinging shutter. The man kissed the woman. She did not move. She stood staring straight in front of her, then her left hand let the hat fall with a drooping, sickly gesture. I hid my head in my hands. No other woman stands as still as Genevieve. Genevieve. Joshua.

And I looked again, and for the second time the baby moved beneath my breasts. I waited.

I went back home immediately. I made myself a fire with nervous haste, the way one does when one needs a barrier of everyday gestures to reassure oneself. I put up my hair in a series of different styles, holding the mirror in one shaking hand. Doing that reminded me of how Joshua had laughed behind me one morning, and of how I had loved that shy and unexpected laugh. Why should I already be having memories of him? We were still together. My eyes fell on some handwritten copies of dissertations. Joshua's writing was a tempest. I loved that writing, as I loved Joshua's hands. I read a few sentences at random: "Man is a being that God has no wish to save." And "Hope comes only with death." There was also an exercise book containing isolated thoughts and some unfinished poems. I fell upon these lines:

Inside you, half asleep, is the child
My soul has made.

His soul. And his body? With rebellion in my heart, I understood that Joshua's body was now in flight, away from me and toward a dangerous reef of dreams.

Genevieve. Joshua. When my eyes have seen something real, I haven't the strength to confront it. I forget it in the thoughtlessness of the moment. Joshua has come in. Does he know what waiting means?

"Aren't you asleep yet. Yance?"

"I was thinking about our child."

He is there. His smell, the cold on his clothes. He's there. I can feel his frozen hand on my eyelids.

"I'll sit by your bed."

"No, do some work, I want to watch you. It's two whole days since you've been here."

He kisses my hands, nibbles gently at the ends of my nails, and then with a supple movement stretches out beside his books. I can see a vein pulsing along his perfect neck.

He puts his hands on the white paper. It is late. Only half of him has come back.

Suddenly, like the beginning of some mysterious lament, I can hear Genevieve's song. I blush. Genevieve hasn't sung for a long while now. Joshua looks at me with candid eyes.

"Perhaps she's coming back to life!"

I open my mouth in supplication, but the words are stifled before I speak them. I kiss his forehead. Everything is laid waste inside me.

Genevieve is still wearing her hair in her mourning style. The woman who took off her hat in the park had let her hair down to her shoulders. So it was only a vision. The apartment is bright and shining; Genevieve takes pleasure in the unreal body that she is becoming. She remains doggedly down there in the depths of herself where Nicolas still talks to her. I am nothing to her at all.

She amasses piles of impeccable shirts, irons white sheets, all this no doubt part of an austere rite whose significance is beyond me. When everything has taken on the whiteness of death, when Genevieve herself has become impregnated with its imaginary purity, then her spirit will relax at last. And the harmony in this house is too frozen. I have the feeling that I too am being drawn, despite myself, into that suspect world, that I too am in love with the ambiguity of irreparable tragedies. I am standing on the brink of a precipice and waiting in patience for the landslide that is to bury us all. Because of this, when I go back to my own life, humbler in its reality, more resigned to the wretchedness it contains, a life made up of Joshua and his desires, it takes me a certain time to detach myself again from Genevieve's gentle, clinging mist. I find myself understanding more and more what Raphael means when he says: "Yance, we have been summoned by death, we are in love with death in this family. That is our misfortune."

I prefer to think that this resignation to nothingness has possessed other souls too, before ours.

Like my thoughts, my dreams are full of anguish. On these June nights, while Joshua prepares for his exams, thin-faced and nervous, I languish through the shuddering darkness. My nightmares are full of Joshua and Genevieve.

One night I dreamed that Genevieve was lying in a bed of flowers, her hair loose about her as when she was a young woman and the object of all my childish concentration: at her neck, against the delicate flesh, and around her wrists as well, there shone bracelets of thorns. In this dream I was vaguely aware that these thorns had the same meaning as her white starched collar and shining cuffs. Someone had laid my sister down in the garden and she had stayed there without moving ever since. She was between death and dying. Suddenly the flowers she was lying on withered, and Genevieve was surrounded by stalks that curved down and held her there. She still did not wake up.

A man came into the garden. Joshua. He came slowly toward Genevieve, knelt down beside her, and cut through the stalks with his teeth. Genevieve allowed her eyelids to be kissed; she suffered Joshua's presence.

When I awoke, the silence I sensed in the apartment made me dizzy. I couldn't hear Joshua's steps in the dining room. Remembering my dream, I ran out into the garden. I recognized that salt taste on the wind, as though it were blowing in from the sea. Genevieve was sitting beside Joshua as he kissed her hands, her forehead, her flowing hair. I opened my arms to the night. The suddenly tilting ground came to my rescue: I fell into a welcome swoon.

And now, this morning, he is still sitting beside me, holding my wrist as though I were some quarry that must not be allowed to escape.

"Are you in pain?"

"It's the baby," I say.

"I'll stay in all day and make you better."

I listen to his words. Is he really being unfaithful to me? Already? And there, in front of me, with that square lock of dark hair shadowing his eyes, is he really nothing but a dream? I think: "As a pregnant woman, I have hallucinations." And then I feel a great haste to be delivered of the child, to be able to press it to my heart and be wholly a woman. And then again I feel a kind of certainty that I did see Genevieve and Joshua out in the garden, just as I felt a certainty earlier, that I had caught them together in the park.

"I'm going to send for the doctor. You're burning hot. Where does it hurt?"

"I'm not in pain."

My voice is no longer my voice. I feel myself becoming as pitiless as my doubts. Yes, I mistrust Joshua, I mistrust his gentleness, which is only the outward shell of his hypocrisy, of his laziness. What if his love were a caprice? (Innocent Joshua . . .)

No, he isn't innocent. But who am I to judge him? His wife, yes; we sleep in each other's warmth, yet I don't feel I have the right to force my way in and occupy the whole consciousness of this untamed lover that my body knows better than my soul. I cannot perceive anything in myself worthy to judge the thoughts of my life's companion in the balance.

There is nothing I blame him for, but I am afraid. Joshua is so eager to be unfaithful to me. But in doing so he envelops me in a tranquil pain, a pain that is the betrayal of our youth. And yet he knows that I am vulnerable, with him as well as without him. What I feel inside me is not just pure jealousy but the swell of an approaching storm as I contemplate my future and that of my husband. Our lives are interlocked in other ways: at moments they meet without being aware of one another.

It is October again.
I have had my baby.
Joshua has begun his third year of Philosophy and is working badly. His vacation was weighed down by my presence. Our silences weigh equally in the scale, our sleeps are wretched and sad. I no longer know if we love one another, but doubtless the birth of our daughter will bring some sort of renewal, inwardly at least.

I feel I want to die of compassion when I look at the tiny thing they hold up above my wounded limbs: I feel pity for a lament that is my own wretchedness. Joshua unveiled the meaning of this emotion when he said to me: "Your face has never been so beautiful, Yance, but it is happy and unhappy at the same time." I sense myself very close to the soft and intimate disengagement of death, as though I have made some sudden break with suffering and shame.

I see all the colors of life when I look at my baby's body. Her future thoughts, her loves, her hopes. Loves that might well resemble mine, and hopes that might well prolong my own existence in that of another. And also a wordless confidence in the power of a time that I shall experience only through her. Cruel and voracious life in which fate has already decided the world of tomorrow! From my breasts to my entrails I am a woman dispossessed.

The child pushes its head down between my opened fingers. The warm void inside me is a thing of pain. They have torn out the little bundle that had nourished itself so well and strongly. Yet this severed life is puny enough at my breast, since it is seeking for itself through me, like a shape that has lost its way. I give it a cool place in the hollow of my being, now wholly without substance. I hear Raphael's words as I told him that I was expecting a child: "Yance, what an idea, to bring a child into the world! Have you any faith in this world? There's going to be a disaster. For us, there is nothing left but the blind present, blind loves, thoughtless pleasures. We have set up our future in one tiny, tormented moment of time. We are the generation of death."

What was the point of that conversation leading no-where? What bad taste, indulging in tragedy like that; and what purpose can such revelations of the future serve? I accept each day quite simply. I love each one as it comes. I love the balance between dawn and dusk, and the chaste sensuality of the nights. I don't think about when I shall be thirty, or when Joshua will be thirty. That has nothing to do with us now. We shall be different people then, we shall be living another life. That's all I feel. I prefer to take refuge in silence.

The child against my heart, Raphael's questioning of the future, and the present have become my whole life. I no longer have confidence in the generation my daughter bears beneath her innocent forehead. A night with no awakening takes shape before me: are we under sentence of death? Are we the shadowy generation chosen to witness the end of the world? Are my doubts simply the presentiment of an ineluctable horror? Raphael is cynical out of fear. Joshua is weak for the same reason. Is it simply a ridiculous panic at the thought of his own death? His own wretched little death? It is true that young people of our generation suffer from their progress through an age of destruction. They suddenly decide they would prefer to live in no age at all. With open eyes, they plunge into gulfs on a scale with their dreams.

Our parents' dying while we were still children prevents us from discussing the terror of our whole generation. I suddenly feel a great sense of gratitude, owed to no one in particular, for having grown up in such great solitude.

(Joshua, Joshua, don't you realize that it's your child I am holding in my arms? Joshua?)

"What are you thinking about?"

"It is a serious thing . . . a life."

"But I'll keep watch over you both."

Yes, he'll keep watch over us. But no more. Joshua has

no faith, he has no life, but he keeps watch over life, he waits to see. And doubtless he is keeping watch over Genevieve in the same way, forgetting that I ought to be the only woman available to his already fragile love. He will never learn to be a father.

(Roxane, my little daughter, Roxane what have we done? Here you are in this world and we shall have nothing to offer you but dreams.)

Yes, I curse all those dreams that will come into Joshua's mind, shattering his reality and the reality of our child.

"Yance, are you crying?"

And there is no tenderness in me any more . . .

November.

There is a nurse in the house taking care of the baby. I am resting. Sometimes I go with Joshua to a lecture. But going back to school is only an attempt to find myself again, an attempt to renew contact with a fictitious freedom. I am cutting myself off from Raphael, who despised me through my confinement; I want to cut out the crazed part of my memory that does not know if Genevieve is a monster or a lost woman. But, back at the university, I am disenchanted. The world has changed. Its dimensions have become more physical, too feminine: I search for the universe I used to inhabit, but the woman in labor is still too fresh inside me. I can think of nothing but the salutary rending of my delivery.

I am no longer a child. Languid and dreamy, I sit beside Joshua as he listens to the teachers and asks questions during the lectures, and I think to myself that I have always known all the human answers before him. The somber mathematics of his brain no longer hold any attraction for me. Before, I would have listened to Joshua with timid admiration, my heart would have felt a tender respect for his haughty and clumsy confidences to the other students. But now I am a woman. There is no more to be said.

Yesterday I was gazing at Joshua's beautiful face; suddenly he thrust his chin into the palm of one hand, so that the spread-eagled fingers covered his cheeks: he seemed to be sunk in humble reflection. I found that I was no longer dreaming as I observed those shifting features; I was penetrating into the depths of their mysteries, I knew them too well. And I no longer felt timid in front of this companion of my flesh.

At this moment of my life I have no one but myself to direct my hopes.

In the evening I come back to life a little for Joshua, as we come back home. He makes a fire, and the sputtering flowers in its flames, echoed by every shadow and every wall, reawaken within me the long evenings we had together during the first September of our adventure. We were happy. Now we aren't. As Raphael blasted the hope of his first love, in his haste to live and to die, so we have put an end to our first youth. It has lost its original, touching grace. And this hour of our life is too lucid to spare us that knowledge.

Silently I rock my baby. Joshua writes, reads, grows tired, goes out and does not come back till late into the night. We don't look at the frozen garden. Its high iron fencing turns the trees into prisoners, and perhaps—those two passionate ghosts as well . . .

As dawn breaks, I often wake up in the grip of an intense melancholy. My little daughter lies asleep between us. Joshua's peaceful face is turned toward me. For an instant, my love flames up anew; I raise my lover's head toward me and kiss the silent lips I had abandoned.

"Genevieve, here is my little girl!"
I hold the baby out toward her. Genevieve gets up, and I seem to see the flood of energy that has been absent from her veins and flesh for so many months rise up in her again. I am shaking because of the baby lying so quietly between my hands. I feel I am saying: "Genevieve, you have tried to bury us all beneath your dead weight of grief, but look, I am stronger than your memories."

Genevieve is smiling. She opens her arms. My pride drains out of me and I feel the humility of her empty arms pressing down upon me like a weight. I lay the baby in the embrace awaiting it. I am very close to Genevieve, I can hear her quick breathing mingled with a warm murmuring sound I cannot understand; I can see the quivering of her bared temples and follow the caress of her fingers over the baby's forehead. It is she who is filling me with wonder now. At last, Genevieve is there before me, and her eyes are no longer dead pools of color, twin lenses focussed on her fear. Her eyes are alive and full of love.

Why hasn't Genevieve become a woman like other women?

A woman who gives herself to a man and is initiated by him?

The sleeping child had closed his eyes,
The child I love was in a dream
And did not see the dying day.

The lullaby begins again, slowly, sweetly. It wells up from some mysterious spring of love. When I take the baby back, my sister doesn't understand. Her hand falls heavily to her side. And the baby searches for my breast with its little outstretched head. Even with such a tiny spark of life inside us, we are already so anxious to satisfy our hunger.

Has Genevieve come back to life? Perhaps. And yet, in the threshold of that room, there is still a girl who has been deceived by her hopes . . .

I am feeding my baby. Joshua, you have turned away your head, because you know that this is the most secret moment of all for me: you are motionless at my feet. Your life, my life, they are being sucked out of us, drop after drop, by a tiny baby's body. Was it you who made me so much a woman? Who brought me into such subjection to the thirst of this young mouth? I love you in this child and I love this child in you. This evening I shall lay my head against your chest, I shall embrace you as though we were newly betrothed.

I am too calm. Come nearer. Take my fullness. That is all that remains inside me now.

"Why are you telling me this, Raphael?"

He talks and talks, and I become the witness of his life, as I am of Genevieve's life, as I was of Nicolas's death. I wish I could feel the unhuman peace of the animals, or simply the uncaring repose of the sick. (Raphael, Raphael, I see your soul as a black torrent. Take it away, out of my sight.)

"Yance, I've found Marie-Christine again, but there is a blight upon her."

"Marie-Christine. Is she an actress now, as she wanted to be?"

"Marie-Christine is blighted, I tell you."

He doesn't know what he is saying. He abandoned her. He doesn't know what it was he did. He has come here to reproach Marie-Christine for giving herself when it was he who taught her to, at a time when she was too young to experience desire. Can he really not remember how he himself awakened that body to love, or the future unconsciously implied in his actions?

"Listen, I'm going to take her back; yes, and she will belong only to me."

"Marie-Christine is an actress at the Théâtre de Vigne, that's all I know. They say she travels about a good deal.

"And did you know that she has lovers, out of caprice?"

And that surprises him. What about him? Wasn't it a caprice on his part, that first untrusting affair? A forbidden freedom that he captured and tamed?

"I spoke to her at the theater. She had that arrogant look you see in girls who have been toughened by life. She laughed. There was a young man standing beside her, looking at her with the eyes of a man who is sure of a woman."

I don't want to know all this. It has nothing to do with my life. I stare at the wall. Night is coming. I avoid my brother's eyes and try not to hear his troubled breathing: soon all our struggles will have returned to the void. I shall no longer have a husband, my child will be far away from my arms, and I shall live in a unique detachment like the sovereign absence of all desire.

"Yance, aren't you my sister any more?"

"Perhaps I am. We're older now."

I close the door behind me and my brother's words are lost inside him like futile winds that struggle among themselves across the sandy shore.

Back at home, Joshua has gone to sleep on the floor. I need him.

"Talk to me."

I cried the words aloud, and my cry drove out the desire that was pressing too hard in my body. I am suddenly aware that I am going to be taken.

"I'll put some wood on the fire. It's cold."

"No, stay where you are."

And it is I, with my two outstretched hands, who bend to imprison that chest and those shoulders; it is my mouth that brushes his damp eyelids: soon we shall be caught up together in the same drunken joy and we shall have forgotten the cold piercing our naked limbs.

It is already several months since my daughter was born. Without warning, I am rediscovering Joshua as a lover. I love his worried head against my body. Like so many married women, I had begun to lose the lover in the husband. Now I am finding my way back to him. Joshua makes love to me as often as he likes, and I love to be taken.

But our love is still on the verge of dying . . .

Genevieve comes back to life when I put the baby in her arms. Like those trees that feed on sun and shade by turns, she adapts herself to a brief and dreaming spell of health, then sinks back into her private shadows. My husband is tired as soon as his need for solitude wells up in him. When Joshua finds his way instinctively to the house, it is simply to make love to the comrade in me, and to forget who I am: he laughs that forced laugh I know so well, always the first sign of his boredom.

What if Joshua no longer knows how to tear himself away from me? I am becoming demanding; I set limits to his life, I exhaust him with my presence. He is a hunted being. He no longer comes to be with me, he is stripping himself of all will. In the spring he failed his exams. Yet it didn't seem to worry him. He was absorbed by some other grief.

This evening we are together and drinking. We are both powerless to live; but as he is now, sitting opposite me, haggard, transfigured by his own searing thoughts, I like him better than when he was always bent over his books as though pondering some irreducible secret.

"Joshua, you're not happy with me."

He doesn't answer. He takes another drink.

"I won't expect you any more in the evenings."

He tries to take me in his arms. No. I refuse to be wounded.

"Come back in a month. Think it over."

Soon there will be the nostalgic calm that fills a body once it is abandoned. But this evening I shan't be his.

He has done as I told him. He has not been back for a month. I had become accustomed to separations of two or three days, but I had no idea how bitter waiting could be, real waiting that has ceased to count the days on its fingers.

I walk through the town and I think to myself that it's absurd to take leave of a man's body when you know it and love it so well. My flesh drifts with the stream, my soul is unable to forget, and I no longer think about my child. There is only Joshua and me. And we are engaged in a false life. Joshua thought he loved me because he desired me. I won't go back to school any more. And I won't wake up any more to find myself weeping for someone who will not come. And all those wild embraces disappearing beneath the flow of time . . . all those embraces that had our identity, the enchantment of our pleasures and the violence of our words. Why? I detest Joshua. I ought to despise him. And how loathsome this courage tastes on the tongue!

I said: "You are free." As he begins dying in me, so his past mistresses will become strangely alive for him again. Walking through the streets of town, I envy the beings who do not belong to the same existence as myself. I envy all those who have not yet set their feet into the stream of time, beings still unfinished within their own untouched plenitude: the children I see. I feel regret at not being the adolescent in a red skirt and black stockings who is laughing as she leans on the arm of a boy her own age, without knowing that she will be alone soon, as soon as she is a woman. I think of the diabolical dimensions that the world will assume for her one day.

But the little girl I am observing without her knowledge, the child full of a thousand hidden dramas, whom I make into the image of my own life and perhaps into the image of my own daughter tomorrow, she passes her days happily today, at home with her thirteen years. She doesn't know if she is still young enough to play ring-around-a-rosy with the younger children, or if she ought to feel herself a woman already, because a boy is stroking her hand. And because there is no choice yet in her life, she is able to do both; she drops her books and dances, then comes back to the boy and stirs his soul with a look whose amorous depths she cannot even gauge herself.

Inwardly, I am separated from that little girl by a whole century. For inside me I can sense a violent and hallowed universe forever seeking the moment to engulf and overwhelm me.

"Good evening, you're all shining in the rain!"
He is there before me. I am lost. Being sundered from him taught me too much. The bonds of absence unknot themselves inside me. As each day of waiting flows into the next, one sinks into a state of bland indifference that is itself another form of wounded love.
"You seem so tall this evening."
"And you so tiny," he replies.

Then we are silent. This night, like all the others, has brought me back a man who will later leave again. And he will have made himself a habit with me.

"The baby?"

"With Genevieve."

This night is also a flood of light illuminating our lost happiness. Our sensuality, as diffuse as our misery, has something in it that lulls my mind, something unreal, an insubstantial spell floating my body into a gentle weariness.

"Are you asleep?"

Yes, let him sleep this evening. I won't make him share my pain and revolt. I love the humility of his repose.

What is there still possible between us? The past, perhaps.

Joshua has been living in the luxury of his sadness for so long.

There must be no succumbing. I am resigned to the enjoyment of small happinesses.

Joshua is asleep.

Before everything ends between us, we shall find our beginning. Perhaps we haven't even begun to exist at all yet.

Just at the moment when I asked Joshua to take our three lives in his hands, he sank from me into sickness. Sickness revolts me as much as death. With Joshua I know that it is more than a lie: it is despair. The fever rises into his eyes like the waves of a nightmare dredging ugliness up from the abyss. The boy I knew before enjoyed happy and simple good health. I wish I knew how to win it back again. But his tongue can taste fevers that are strange to me: the man I hold against my heart is not Joshua. In the delirious eyes of the man I love, I see my life breaking free from me. Probably I am not the sort of woman to whom it is possible to give oneself forever. I thought as much.

Like Genevieve gripped by her tenacious passion, by her desire to save Nicolas, I am capable of tearing everything inside me to shreds, of losing everything, in order to drag Joshua from these long, feverish suicides. Nothing could be more in conformity with his nature than this monstrous abandon to his delirium! He wants this sort of oblivion. I will not let him have it.

Joshua has never belonged to me. He is a god of darkness and secret deliriums, not a man who possesses a woman. He is a thousand vague and delicious things, but not a responsible human being. He shares the madness of all children born without an age to live in, the protean changes of all such youthful exiles.

I have felt a flame of life at my waist, I have listened to the whole soul of a child beating in my veins, and love in my heart; I am alive, healthy, and reasonable in my fashion, but Joshua is a receding series of reflections, darkness dissolving into ghosts: he stands beside people and things, but without knowing them. He lives in perpetual flight. He came to me with the intention of drawing me away with him into his own world of mists and dangerous fantasies; he caressed my body with innocent hands, yet I should have known from the very beginning how that innocence would come to kill me, that innocence more treacherous than any evil spell. Oh! sick child far from my heart! Oh young man, disarmed and gazed at now with eyes full of tears! As I lean down and look into Joshua's indifferent face, I know that I did not choose him but that he chose me for the worse. The young man from the shadows, irresistible because of that inhuman candor, will leave me nothing but a house of scents and dreams, little, very little that is real: he will leave me a little girl as insubstantial as he himself is, a flower made of nothing but a little dew.

After coming as a stranger, the man of illusions has returned for his own self-destruction. I shall wait.

"Hear me, Joshua, I shall wait . . ."

We shall live through a few more carefree days, but they will be days of convalescence . . .

"Joshua, it's summer. We ought to leave this town and go to Black Island. You'll get better there, I know you will."

It was on Black Island that our adventure together first began—once upon a time. An unexplored time, full of discoveries and beginnings: the budding of a boy's ephemeral modesty, of passion incapable of expression, then of the love that knows nothing yet of hands or bodies.

I grew up free, like Joshua, who lay moodily on the seashore from morning till night. But then I suddenly felt a desire for the reality of life and for my own reality as a responsible child, whereas Joshua never accepted any world other than the changing, innocuous life of the beaches, the rhythm of the sea. Since then there have been two worlds inside Joshua: the world as all men imagine it, and that visionary world of his childhood. But one of those worlds was unable to find its rightful place, and it has slaughtered everything around it.

We are leaving for Black Island. My daughter already spends more time with Genevieve than with me, so I shall not take her back on the vacation. Immersed as I am in the anguish of having a husband to love, my little girl moves me—but in too distant a way. She takes on the transparency of a piercing memory, the image of a desire too completely fulfilled. Perhaps I shall return to her again afterward, but she must still allow me a great deal more time. I don't belong to her—just as Joshua doesn't belong to me. I brought her into the world too soon, before I knew anything about it.

When Roxane was born, Joshua said: "This baby's body was created by an angel." No, he has no sensation of that flesh being his, of its having come from him. He looks up from depths of his dreams and he does not recognize her. Realizing this makes me hard and rebellious because before, when I knew instinctively how to be a mother, I taught myself how not to be.

Now we prefer the chaos of bright beaches. It is here that we have chosen to act out this first termination of ourselves. In all the everyday details of our lives here we are stupidly young.

We walk in the sunlight across landscapes that our troubled glances scarcely touch. And then there are the train trips, the railroad stations where we hope to find an oasis. Whenever a sudden fever burns up in my husband's cheeks, I think: "The unknown sickness, the dream, his dream." And I am jealous. In the vulnerable silence of these journeys together, I find that my husband resembles some long, gray animal idly anxious to slip away into the morning mist. Then he looks like a child. Even his body has something too naked and too sensitive about it that I can only compare to the quivering beauty of young children's bodies.

And what I desire in him is the man. The strong man who will make my soul explode within me, with a single word. There is the dreamer, his hand lying open on his knee, and he is waiting for another woman, he too . . .

PART TWO

And yet love, which is a coupling of egos,
will sacrifice everything to itself and lives on lies.

R. Radiguet, *Le Diable au Corps*

Black Island.

The country where this man I love grew up, loved, and
lived. I have had a dream about that summer when we slept
in hay, sang as we fished, and met a whole crowd of irre-
pressible young people who came every year to bring
Black Island back to life.

After a few nights, I sensed in Joshua that patient
warmth that ravishes a woman's body. And I came to
replace his fever, like an adored illusion. And after a few
days too, we began to go out for walks again along the wet

57

sands; our hands and our feet were recognizing the marks they had left during that first summer.

Joshua still keeps the greater part of himself reserved for his unquiet dreams. In my passion, I long to tear out the poisoned thorn that lies dormant inside him. If he would only give himself to the summer! But it is too long now since he ceased to be pure. He has to have his mysterious companion, his wandering melancholy. Often, as we come back from swimming, hand in hand, Joshua turns to look at me with the ravaged face of a desperate man. My eyes can find no way to smooth out that face. Then there are silences as hurt as our two selves. (He's an angel, a monster, a gambler.) But then my sadness vanishes, and I forget the pain I have just felt.

We walk through the woods in dawns wet with dew, my head on my husband's shoulder. We are forgetting our two lives in an easy existence, warm as fruit.

Now the last days of the vacation are upon us, I feel I am being wrapped in a vague darkness. I close my eyes to tomorrow. It is coming, like the fall mists, and it clutches at my stomach like a death summons.

It is seven o'clock. Joshua has loved me all night on the shore. I am beginning to feel sleep steal over me, but it is a smooth, unbroken sleep in which my body knows that it is understood: my heart is beating confidently inside my flesh. This is something new to me. I still haven't tasted all the sleeps that love can bring. But now, now begins the slow spread of the mist over the sea. A still mist that wells up furtively from the waves. Joshua stands up and looks at the mist. His gaze is beautiful and sweeping; he has never looked at me in this way.

"Let's go in, Joshua."

He doesn't understand. He is gazing at the sea of mist.

Eight o'clock, and the mist has enveloped the beach now; just as it enveloped Joshua's steps and his slow-moving, untamed body a little while ago. He won't come back to me now. My presence is no more than a breath of wind. I cannot prevent him any longer from walking, from escaping, from dying. He isn't mine. He was expected in this refuge of shadows. He has found mistresses of sand, and the limitless void.

Nine o'clock. Joshua is coming back. He emerges from the mist and shakes his head with a laugh. He is reassuring himself.

"When I was little, I used to go for long walks in the mist. Why didn't you follow me, Yance?"

"And what did you see out there?"

"Shadows."

I clutch at his hand.

"But you're crying. Always a little girl. Sobs and tempers, but never despair!"

Oh, yes, my darling, how right you are. Like a little girl. But at last, despair . . .

I open my arms and squeeze him to me so hard that it hurts my chest. He laughs; he sings out the unforgettable laugh, the vibrations that will always ring against my temples. I recognize the sharp scent of fever on Joshua's lips. The sickness is alive in him again. And I am dying.

"Take me back to town, Joshua. Tomorrow."

"Yance. What is it you're so afraid of?"

"I want to go back to town."

Just as there are fevers that come and go according to the rhythm of a journey, so there are words and thoughts that judge and sentence us according to the rhythm of our lives.

Joshua, I am here waiting for your fever to end, and I say to you: "Talk to me now, because tomorrow we shall part."

Yes, you are free of me. Will you admit that you are rejecting me for your shadows? I am keeping vigil over your death, and your enemies have surrounded us. I am being cut down as a field of wheat is cut down with a scythe. I have loved your mind and your body to the point of madness: the humblest thought you ever thought for me has fed me with eternal hope, and today I love your mind and body in repose. To my eyes' tenderness your arms are the most majestic in the world when they are no more to you than simply two clumsy and shaking limbs. I have loved your forehead and I have believed in noble thoughts that perhaps you never had. Who will do all that in my place? You are agonizingly innocent. But of what use is it, my love, to be innocent in that way and yet lack the strength to belong to a woman? I no longer wish to carry your weight. Go. But what will become of you? I was always there. I was your guide. Like the ineluctable glow that one can scarcely make out through the darkness. And I myself, without you I shall be more naked still. Freedom is a tragic thing, and you are too weak for it. Joshua, how I love you and how I pity you! Joshua, Joshua, I am your wife. Do you remember me?

"Listen, Joshua . . ."

Yance, my wife, I am leaving you. I no longer feel able to be close to you. What peace we shall both know, my dear one, when our struggles have been torn apart! I could wish so much to be yours in the way that you are mine, but I have not made any choice yet, and I shall not know how to choose tomorrow. What I require is an obedient illusion that invents its forms anew each day, as a landscape does; what I require is your soul as my traveling companion, Yance, your soul, yes, but you, that lucid body with its vast and supplicating gaze, unyielding Yance, stripping me of my dreams so that you can come to life in your brief moments of cold passion, you are made of all that I am not, and I cannot follow you.

"Joshua, you are my husband."

She has brought me to this island in order to relive the memory of our happiness when we were still fifteen.

I can no longer talk to her because I no longer belong to her. Can it be that you are passing judgment on me, Yance? I didn't choose the mists: the mists came to me. I grew up in the living dream of the sea, I grew up with the fishermen who hold the sky-filled waters in their weather-beaten hands; I have touched the shadows and I know them. Are you to pass judgment on me, you who have lived in the cities? You who have known thick walls and the muteness of their houses? You who come from the noise of the cities with your sure step.

When one is a son of the waters and the sands, there is no turning from the summons of the wind. I lived on my island until I was thirteen. Later I saw the cities gape before me like wounds. And you were there. I said: "Let us go back and live in my country." And you laughed, and you were already too sure of me. And of everything, Yance.

I am a man who is leaving his wife for a childhood of mists. And that is not good. But how does one belong to an age, or a woman? I should be ungentle, too gentle, one or the other. Or I should become violent and betray the yearning for infinity that has me in its grip. And that is something that does not belong to her. Wife, Yance, sister, who am I?

I opened my eyes and sensed your profile quivering beneath the lamp. The lamp. The lamps. There were too many lamps in our old Black Island house. And in our house in the town, we had bought a great many lamps too, trying to recapture the magic of times past. The blue lamp in our bedroom. The gray lamp on the piano. The lamp with its mournful reflections beside the fire. And the desk lamps that you came and lit when I came in from classes. Your thin arm as I squeezed it then—and you smiling. You would disappear again immediately. I listened to your footsteps on the stairs every evening.

(The first summer on Black Island.)

Where are the burning sands, and the paths, and the

huge rocks? And where is the happiness, tell me that, Yance, tell me that . . .

"Don't forget the child. Have you thought about the child?"

No.

It was you who wanted the child, and I admired the beauty of your wish. I have loved the child. But though I love with all my heart, I don't yet know how to love. It is as though nothing is precious to me, really. If I could explain it to you, you would understand. You have understood everything I have inside me. Tomorrow we shall both be alone.

I look at your face, Yance, and I see in you again the girl of sixteen. All one saw was her eyes. Black, their fire too heavy for the eyes of a child. I don't remember her hair. Brown and black and very supple in a man's hands. When the child was born, Yance became slightly more shadowy. I have forgotten her eyes and her hair.

The reality of the mists is more alive than all other realities. In the world of flesh, I bruise and am bruised in return. In life, I cannot find my rightful place. Yance, will you take pity on me? Will you let me go?

"You can go when you like."

She hears everything.
The summer we were sixteen . . . I held your knees

between my hands. To me, that gesture signifies the first leaves falling from a body. I stripped the leaves from your two knees, Yance. I tasted your muscles with my tensed fingers. A woman who has been loved knows so many things. A man who has loved is suddenly wounded by a light as carnal as hunger.

She brought me here to Black Island so that she could find out how to revive a man who has been killed. I wasn't completely absent. I still watched her living sometimes. And I lived with her, to please her, obeying a rhythm that is utterly strange to me.

This crazy girl of mine has been harboring a hope as unreasonable as the sea. In exchange, I offered her my evasions. Why did I bind myself to her? To her footsteps? To her teeth held captive in a kiss? I believed I would never now return to being the boy of ashes that I am, so vague in outline, miscarried deep inside himself, at once despairing, yet full of laughter.

I thought: "Take the woman of flesh and blood." We made love in the woods, on the sands, on the rocks; I possessed that body everywhere, and she gave way to me, yielding herself up to every shipwreck. Why should she be mine, this little golden girl lying against my side? Why should I be her eternal ravisher?

At the end of our two different roads, I know that she will be there, perhaps in twenty years, perhaps in ten years, with open arms . . . And I shall love her at last.

"Open your eyes and look at me."

There is so much courage in her love, and it is with this fleshly love that she carries on her struggle, still trying to support me in my weakness. She is standing up. Her steps are trampling through the fog of my thoughts. Yes, let her come to me.

"Drink."

I feel her fingers against my damp cheek. I love her fingers. She knows it. I can smell the scent of ink on her fingers. She has driven the fever out from my body. She is trying to give me the sunlight of a thought.

The unfinished summer. Our unfinished love. Black Island was a country that reflected all our youth. The shames of the great shameful towns were lulled to sleep in the ebb and flow of our anxieties. The industrial towns. And the sensual towns that ought to live only by night. Black Island was our Daylight Isle.

She is kissing my forehead. Then my lips. I desire her, but it is an obscure desire that has no weight. And she is weeping. She mustn't weep. Make yourself used to the thought that I might no longer exist. I have never got into the habit of being. Oh, be good now, wipe away your tears with the ends of your hair, my poor trampled reed!

Yes, we had this island, and the abandoned houses, and the woods, and the little scented coves where you went to sleep in my arms. So many, many birds on this island! I remember. In the morning, you rolled about on the big white bed and you sang a song of desire, between your teeth:

My love stroked my body to sleep with his right hand,
My lover caressed my shoulders . . .

Sing. Sing. We walked down naked to the sands and I
took your head between my hands as soon as you began to
think of anything that was not me. And I would take you,
Yance, as soon as you began to think of me too much. Sing.
Sing, Yance. In those days you were only a child with
empty breasts and a hollow belly, a child as you sang a
woman's song! I can see that child even now, warm as the
salt on the stones, warm as the print of her elbow in the
flaming sand.

"And the jellyfish . . ."

Sing, Yance.

I see Yance now. The short hair, the neck that was too
long and dazzled me with the beauty of its movements.
The neck of a proud child. She was there, reserved, sensible, and candid in her slightly animal dignity. She fixed
her secrets on the darkening horizon and watched the seaweed on the beaches die.

I see her kneeling on the grass, in the afternoon. A
woman sewing, a woman meditating on a scented garment.
And now and then, without being quite aware of what she
is doing, she presses the shirt against her heart. The gesture
was full of pity for me. Yance, I can see you dancing
through the newly hung-out washing; you kiss me respect-
fully after making love, and you are so vibrant that I
suddenly sense the whole of that quivering miracle you are
heavy with because of me. You love me.

Speak to her. Impossible utterance. I can no longer find the balance for my words. She is waiting. I wish I could bite her lips till I have killed the taste there that I know will follow me. Quickly, close your eyes, Yance.

I shall leave you tomorrow.

PART THREE

The woman looks at the man and says: "My love, I think that this is the end of us now, the true one."

She does not want to know why woe is born of love. Soon she will hear the man running in the rain outside. And she has a presentiment of the irresistible passion that will force her to stretch out her arms to him emptied of all embraces.

"How old are you?"

"Twenty."

Her voice is scarcely harder than it sounded yesterday and less sad than it will be tomorrow.

She savors the thoughts that she will not have for him again. There is a beautiful and clumsy tenderness in those who are about to leave us, as in those who are about to die. It lasts no more than a moment and yet it is fiercely eternal. It is a tenderness utterly untamed.

"And where will you go?"

"I know some coast towns, to the west," he says.

"I know distant cities, too," she says.

She dreads the approaching dawn. She thinks: "I shall be free!" But for her, that freedom carries the weight of a defeat. "He was my poor triumph, and he is leaving me."

"And then, if he needs a whole town to forget, that's something."

But there is also the child they are leaving behind in the big house with Genevieve. (The child of her dream is fading at last.)

"I'll think about my Beloved Dream tomorrow."

Tomorrow. It comes; you think of the man you are leaving. You drive bitterness further and further away from you. There is nothing but the cold nakedness of separation. Then you make haste to try and remember, imagining that you are making haste to forget.

(He is able to reach his shadows; but in me he is flesh: the resistance is too great.)

She says suddenly: "And why do you exist?"

In his dizziness, she has wounded him. Perhaps it is her right, since he is leaving. Since he is giving her the proof that he will never belong to her again.

"But you don't exist, in fact. Not for me."

"I exist as the wind exists. I told you to beware of me," he replies.

Their anger makes them beautiful; they both stand tall suddenly; their eyes are no longer lowered.

"Come with me," the man says. "It is still only evening. Come with me and do as my hands bid you. Afterwards, I will leave you."

"No, I don't wish to obey any more. Everything is over. Go."

This rebellion is the last fruit of their love.

Joshua loves the taste for battle that is dilating Yance's eyes and hardening the sinews of her neck.

The short vein under the locks on his forehead also takes fire. Joshua awakens to a magnificent swell of passion: he thinks of the desire in him that is about to bend back Yance's long, stretched neck.

"Go! Quickly!"

The man takes the woman bereft of speech into his arms and carries her to the bed. Yance still keeps those new eyes of hers, that gaze of somber contempt and fevered boldness.

"You are beautiful," he says.

"How I hate you!"

She is delivered of him. The man laughs and strokes her hair.

"This is how you should be, darling."

He undresses her, overwhelms her with heavy embraces and little moist bites, and she sinks beneath a rising flood of luminous abandon, intent on nothing but the man's undulation against her body. She encloses his deep chant inside her breast. Her belly gently shivers. She glows with the splendor of her secrets and no longer has eyes for her lover. This way, she thinks, he can still go.

He is going. She has not forgotten the humdrum gestures that follow love. The humble hand laid on the shirt or reknotting a tie, the nervous hand brushing back the disordered hair or stroking the tanned cheek. (Darling, your cheeks are the color of the sand. It's true that you come from the northern shores.) She omits nothing. She kisses him on the brow. She drives him out too, when he lingers to look at her, when he lingers to admire the beauty he has just given her.

She drives him out at midnight and she says: "Don't forget to shut the garden gate." And she comes back to her silent room. She has repudiated her youth.

Raphael, Raphael, is it midnight already?
Marie-Christine wishes she could ask him how midnight came so soon; but she remains silent: the man is too close to her heart. Their desire has passed, but it is still hesitating over them, like the sun between two sheets of rain, at dawn.
(Marie-Christine, so near, so cold, consumed and yet so despairingly present.)
"I want to be a great actress, but you must let me go away to some happy country! I don't like this snowy country where I grew up, or the frozen loves that people live here . . ."
"But what about me, Marie-Christine, are you thinking of me?"
"You can come with me."

Raphael listens to the pulse of the woman's wrist against his neck. Before, it was he who said: "You can come with me." And she gave herself up to him in her horror-struck childishness, her childishness already trembling with sensuality. And she could do nothing but submit to him. But she is older now, and she has found in love all the sufficient reasons for her follies, as well as a vagabond life undreamed before.

At twenty, she already looks as she will at thirty. Raphael knows all the masks this body wears; they are so close to his own unbalanced nature.

"Yes, you can come with me, and we'll go live somewhere where I want to live . . ."

Does she know that the man will agree to everything she asks because he possesses her now, and because there is nothing he understands any more except that ecstatic moment in which so many years of his life are to be lost?

"Yes, I'll go with you."

He will go with her so as not to think any more about the disaster obsessing him. He will leave without a backward glance at this country of his, at the snows of this country that he loves; but he knows that he cannot live anywhere else but in this country, which is his, anywhere but in this land to which his thirst for finality and the pain of death has irretrievably committed him.

Raphael returns to an awareness of time and things. He hears the garden gate being opened—and footsteps, and the rain on those footsteps.

"Yes, Marie-Christine, it's midnight already."

PART FOUR

A calm keening wind, unknown to the stars,
Sprung from no point on our charted horizons,
Layered the bay with the low cast of doom.
Our old world is broken, make ready the ships."

Max Jacob

"And where were you?"
"In the mist. Walking."
"I've been waiting for you since dawn."
"Soon you won't have to wait for me."

I am always looking for my wife. Always losing her, in
the woods as well as in the town. She vanishes into many-
faceted evasions that I cannot understand. I am jealous of
all those voiceless things that so absorb her, of those mysterious encounters that she refers to in my presence. How am
I to halt this urge to flight in her? She doesn't laugh any

more. She gazes at the windows as they stream with heat or rain.

"You're a hard man, Jessy."

"Perhaps."

As I sit hunched over my scattered drawings, sometimes I look up at her, spying out the promise in her fingers and the vibration of her tight-shut knees. I wish I could drink the whole of that bewildered profile in one long gulp!

"Ever since I became your wife, Jessy, I feel I have the hands of a slave."

I never draw her face, because it doesn't belong to me. Why is it that after a year of being married she wants to take back all she's given me? I have to watch her drifting away from me like seaweed that seeks the shore.

"And what did you see on the beach?"

"All the things there that are happy and beautiful because they are not human."

How many more times will she tell me that she suffers from having to exist?

She blames me for her own existence. She has passed sentence against me because she says I created her with my love. That first cry as I took her when she was fifteen: "Jessy, it's not that I want to exist: did I ask to be born?"

And now she is eighteen and she is my wife and I have not succeeded in bringing her into the world of the living. I raise my head. She is no longer there. The open door is swinging in the afternoon air. Roxane is running down toward the shore, and the marks of her sandals leave a flowery track wherever she goes.

How black her hair is in the rain! It seems to be wanting to melt into the darkness, indifferent to all caresses. I think of Roxane's hands driving me away.

Her eye is bright with that dreaming fury I have come to dread.

"Come on then, darling, follow me."

And she draws me on in headlong pursuit of her flying feet, of her shadow. She makes herself tall and fluid. For an instant I grasp the whirlwind of her skirts, but she is immediately free again.

I hear that panting voice, a voice even stranger to me than it was before: "Not here, there's too much mud, it's like a swamp."

I don't listen to her. I bite her lips, I bruise her whole body, with the thought that though she may refuse herself to me, still she will not refuse herself to pain or pleasure. I want to feel my dead and heavy arm crushing down against her breasts: she moans, her whole face annihilated and illumined at the same time by fear or a somber need for ecstasy.

"Get up," I tell her.

She gets up without looking at me and looks for her sandals along the edge of the water.

"You hurt my ankles."

We walk back barefoot, one behind the other, nonexistent, unfathomable even to ourselves, like opponents who have gone through the same struggle and suffered the same defeat.

The nights are our salvation. The days lay bare our sufferings with their sunlight. I never paint Roxane's body. I wouldn't know how to give it shape. If ever I do perceive her true form it is in the morning, as she gazes out at the mists, so still and distant that I quickly make myself despise her.

"But what is it you are looking for in those accursed mists?"

"What am I looking for, Jessy? The way back to where I came from."

"You came from life as I did, as all the beings on this earth did."

"I feel that I was born like a dream, in a dream . . ."

I am twenty. I am trying to find out who Roxane is, to penetrate her veils of sleep.

"Who is your father? You never talk about him."

"He may be dead. He seems not to exist. I never knew him. And my mother probably lives in some strange city, like so many women whose husbands have left them."

"You have memories, you had a childhood . . ."

"No. If I had memories, then I would know where I came from and why I seem never to have been summoned by life. I was brought up by an aunt. You know her. Genevieve. You said to me when you saw her: "She might be alive or she might be asleep." She has been thinking about nothing except a dead child for years and years. You know all that, Jessy."

"And you? And you?"

"If I am a part of this world, then perhaps I was sent to reincarnate that child. But I don't want to exist in someone else's place."

Only a little longer and she will break this spell.

I draw the world in around her and around myself, and our youth is transformed into a series of flights and captures. Soon I shall make Roxane share just one room with me. I am like children when they play at life; in my clumsy disillusion I am trying to shut the world up between four walls. To hold a soul prisoner for one instant, what a temptation!

Just this one room to live in and die in. Roxane no longer attempts her sudden escapes into the woods; she is indifferent: a gloomy sleepwalker. She no longer knows how to live with herself. By stripping her of her taste for unreality I have also stripped her of her reality.

An awakening, and our room is crammed with miracles; but my wife is still oblivious of who the lover in her fullness is: she deserts me even in the midst of pleasure.

I can feel no similarity between her soul and mine. I was born of another generation: I am part of mankind. I have abandoned the vast world of dreams for a reality that is the present, that will be the future; or, you might say, I have preferred the humility of everyday things to that nameless lethargy in which Roxane's thoughts are perpetually lost. So that our one room is shrinking around a pitiful discovery. . . .

September is almost upon us.

Soon we shall return to the great city where we live so that I can study. We shall once more find ourselves short of words and space in our little apartment in a student hostel. My friends, my classmates will console me with their living absorption in reality. But Roxane will attach herself to no one. She will swim down alone into her great despair.

October. School.
A passing and sometimes faceless mistress, a bright and illusory flame before boredom returns. And my wife, always there, like a beautiful stranger whom I love, apparently, out of despair.

Yet I am happy when she seems to take pleasure in this world where she lives, this world where we live. When she looks at the bread with joy in her eyes, when she sings as she washes her hair. That is how I try to see her: wearing the features of a humble woman who could be content with the happiness of the days as they follow one another, joyfully . . .

November.
She is expecting a baby. I know she is. I felt the budding, swollen life yesterday. She draws refreshment from her own blood, arms tightly pressed against her belly. She is mistrustful of any power outside that sacred weakness deep inside her body.

"You're expecting a baby."

"But it will never be born. I don't want it to be."

But I do want it, this baby. I want to fix my life in time with the help of that tiny shapeless thing waiting inside her. I won't think of anything but our child, and it will live.

"Jessy, you must cure yourself now, before it happens, of the pain I'm going to cause you! You're not going to have a child."

Roxane avoids me. I can see the pain at her waist and the revolt in her clenched fists. Her mind wants to lose the child but her flesh will love it.

Before next autumn, before the season of pain, before the end of the world, I shall have a son.

The snow. I am no longer a student. I am a father-to-be and a lover-to-be, and I know that everything has to be begun all over again. With Roxane, I live in expectation of the man who will trample my dark adolescence underfoot.

I can no longer paint: I am in some new, unexplored region of my own spirit. My blood is renewing itself, my nerves dazzle me with their extreme feats of endurance. I am about to discover a world for myself and a soul for the child that is coming. The snow is here. Hard and fine, as hard as the white world of nature that has us in its grip. We have left the city for the winter. My wife will be able to rest better here, on the fringes of these deserted woods. I knew that we were about to be given a priceless new world.

Roxane walks beside me. I think of the child as we plunge our advancing feet into the muffled whiteness of the snow.

"You know, Jessy, I was sincere about not wanting the baby, and I'm sincere now about wanting it. What was it that changed?"

"You came to see that it is simpler to become a woman than to remain a Shade."

"But what you don't understand is that it's a Shade I have inside me."

Why is she still trying to find justifications for living a lost existence?

"Do you think I did it on purpose then, Jessy? I love you. I should be with you all the time if there weren't something always calling to me—as though I were longing to plunge back into the void. My father must be a great god of fog and clouds. Don't you think?"

How is it possible for a being so completely without a sense of belonging to live? From what rebellious race has Roxane sprung?

I took her in my arms beside the ice-covered tree stump and I kisssed her there in the cold—and this, this, I told her as I wept, should perhaps be termed our first true marriage.

Our winter house. Others have doubtless tried to salvage their love in summertime. But we, we wandered lost and apart from one another in the summer. And it is the season more despair-filled than any other, the black season, the untamed maiden we call winter, that is forcing us into awareness of ourselves. Thus the soul begins to confront the body.

"Can you hear the snow as it melts under my boots, Jessy?"
"Yes, I hear it."
"Can you hear the fire?"
"Yes, I hear it."
"You're hearing everything for the first time."

She makes me think back to the young girl I loved when I was thirteen, in a winter long since dead.

"Have you loved other women, Jessy?"

"Yes."

"Since we were married too, Jessy?"

"Yes."

The fire has flamed up in the fireplace again. The cat has woken up at the far end of the room. Now he is fixing the flames with his round stare. I have already painted the cat's eyes. And Roxane said: "They're hungry eyes."

"But what are they hungry for?"

"They would like to be a man's eyes."

That was at the time of our deepest ignorance. In the summer, by the sea.

Roxane believes that animals unconsciously desire to be men when men consciously desire to be beasts. She makes free with others' souls because she doesn't know what to make of her own destiny. I would like to make myself resist her charm, for it is the charm of death.

The sleeping child had closed his eyes,
The child I love was in a dream
And did not see the dying day.

"What are you singing?"

"The lullaby that Genevieve used to sing to Nicolas."

The child has gathered the gentle tides
Between his pure young hands.

"And that?"

"Genevieve says my father wrote those lines for me."

And she goes on singing:

The child will come back to the house of shades
At winter's dawning,
To the sound of the white flutes of morning
The child will come back to the house of shades.

Her baby quivered suddenly then, in the intimacy of her body. There is nothing I can hold on to.

"Jessy! I am being eaten alive!"

"Speak to me."

She has hidden her face in her hands.

The snow has been falling now for days and nights. Jessy has become a young, wounded man again; his face is vulnerable and candid once more. His mouth has the old disillusion in it, his brow the old revolt. Jessy stands there, outside of things and the absurdity of their gladness, overwhelmed with his own powerlessness. Tomorrow the woman will be sufficiently detached from her suffering to say: "How it snowed yesterday and how the baby hurt me!" But everything will be over by then: the rebellion will have turned to repose; all will be release, and utter stillness . . .

She will have forgotten the spreading blood. She will have grown so old that she will be wholly without age. All her pain would be nothing more than the pain of a humble and humiliated woman, if only she did not have to see it reflected back at her from her husband's face. He no longer hides from her how much she makes him suffer. Love's failure is blazoned now across his mouth.

"Speak to me, Jessy!"

(My love, I shall leave you tomorrow. Or this evening. And you will have to search for your happiness by yourself, and you will find it, I'm sure of it. I am tired of seeing you laid waste because of me. I am leaving you and it is I who cannot find any place in which to live now. But you, you know where to live. You have chosen the easiest country of all: the country of shadows, the country of everlasting day. What is there more for me to wait for, my darling? Other women could no longer reach me inside the man that you have made of me.)

The child will come back to the house of shades
At winter's dawning,
To the sound of the white flutes of morning.

Already we are no longer together. We are apart.

"We have had a bad dream. Is that our fault?"

"Goodbye, goodbye, Roxane, I am already too far away from you to hear."

"Jessy, where are you going?"

"I'm going out. I want to go for a walk through the snow."

"You must be back before six."

"Yes, at five. I shall walk through Swan Forest."

"How it snowed yesterday! How the baby hurt me!"

"I forgot to make a fire. And you're cold."

"Come back before dusk."

"Yes."
"Goodbye then, Roxane."

The man goes out into a cold that pierces his entrails like the breath of God. But it is a vague cold borne on a dry wind. The snow, lying in great drifts across the hill roads and blotting out the footsteps of the little schoolboys with its darkness, has now ceased to fall. It is a day created for the peace of a world that loves nothing but war.

Jessy's need to walk is like a hunger, and his soul now feeds that hunger—a miraculous hunger, an unsought-for gift, a kindly grace to which intelligence must bow.

The snow seeps into his boots and penetrates his clothing. Once upon a time, he used to dawdle on his way home to his parents' house in order to make little snowgirls on the sidewalk.
"Five o'clock, Jessy, you must be back by five."

Five o'clock, the time for punishments. The snow is doing his body good. Yesterday the snow cured his soul. Why should he go back at five o'clock when he wants to see the setting sun across the snow? On punishment days he was never allowed to watch the sunset. His sister used to bring him bread and jam in bed. He smiles. It wasn't so sad after all . . . going in at five o'clock. He can no longer recall his sister's face. He can remember the little brothers who never stopped growing. And he was already so big himself . . . The little brothers his mother used to bathe, all together, on Saturdays and Wednesdays, and the feeling of loneliness that always came over him, on those days.

And how his little brothers stole his pocket money. He can remember the first forbidden books he read while his mother had forgotten him in the younger children's bedroom. Two worlds. Himself, the eldest, then the younger brothers, and no place at all for their ageless sister in that childhood world. The afternoon light is slanting across him, across his footsteps, across the pink snow.

(I could paint again, after all this time.)

He thinks of his student friends in the hostel where he lived during the early part of the winter. His young friends, married or still lovers, adapting to life so easily, full of energy and fervor. He loves them. And they love him too. He has been loved a great deal. He has a vision of all those faces, of all the complex lives that lie behind them.

The road up to the village school. After that, Swan Forest, where the whirling whiteness of the track will come to an end. His feet are burned by the melted snow, and his neck feels cold, just as it did when he was afraid, as a very little boy.

He loves those sad little schoolboys kept from truancy by the cold, lugging along their damp satchels crammed with homework, with tasks as dismal as all winter labors inevitably must be. Heroically, they emerge from the blizzards that have frozen their knuckles along the white-powdered roads, only to dig out and wield those pens and pencils once again. He loves those gloomy urchins wandering into the houses at four o'clock, just as the evening lamps are being lit. Already, insecurity looms, and they dream of long, lazy meals eaten in silence. This evening the schoolboys trudge by him on both sides of the road, and Jessy gazes at them as they pass. In the same way he used to gaze at his own small brothers when he possessed that strange power that older brothers have. Today, as always, he is both the doomed and the favored child.

And then the frozen stream. The mountain on either side, and Swan Forest.

Five o'clock.

Roxane was right. The snow is beginning to melt here. But the forest is so solitary in this evening light. One could fashion such cold, tall virgins here. And watch them melt into eternity. His hands are clenched. He has grown up. A man. How quickly one becomes a man! No, he would never go back to that angular childhood of his . . .

Everything is as it should be. He senses the perfection of the hour and a sort of unfinished perfection present in life. He has no wish to go back to anything, as Roxane wants him to. He has taken all he wanted to take. He is free.

The stream is in flow: he can feel it beneath his feet. A branch bends, there, to the right of his elbow. A silvery tree is stretching its roots out to the dying day, and Jessy seems to hear the flow of a numbed and tawny sap deep, deep inside his head. He listens to the winter birds. Another life is on its way. And that tree; as he leans against it he feels it draping him with mourning. He breathes it deep into his own being. He becomes its heart, he merges with its darkness. Jessy clings to the tree, and the tree supports him. He consents to hang himself. The moment is on its way. The moment has come: the rope is knotted around his neck, the branch already bearing his weight, the blood slowing in its course. The man is up above the snow, the ground falls away. The snow is melting on the bark of the tree, beneath Jessy's lacerated neck, and in his clothes. It is running down the small of his back, between his thighs, dripping onto his heels, mingling with the sweat on his face. And how slowly the blood beats now in his veins! How terribly it struggles!

The forest rises with him. And all the faces he has loved rush down upon him in a fevered avalanche. He understands. He is going to die. This tumultuous agony was his choice. He feels no despair. He understands that his blood is becoming as still as the snow all through his body, he understands that the rope is pulled tight around his neck and that his breath is halted like a stifled cry upon his lips. And it all happened so simply!

He is astonished that he feels no pain, and that his thoughts are not of God. He is bound to this tree, he is bound to God. It is getting too late. Five o'clock. The birds are still singing. The stream is flowing. Jessy wishes he had enough strength to gnaw through the rope with his teeth and throw himself down into that bed of snow. Yes, to put his feet into the stream, as he did a moment ago.

He closes his eyes. Everything has sprung open inside him, a deluge of passions and disorder: his body is deserting him, his blood is abandoning him on every side, his eyes are weeping, his shoulders collapsing; the tree remains upright, solitary, silent.

It is no longer possible for him to set foot on the ground and lock everything up inside himself again: the flesh, the blood, the snow, the mud. He forgets he is afraid. The birds sing and the tree still stretches its naked roots up to the sky.

It is past five o'clock and the young man is dead.

PART FIVE

Marie-Christine.

The man watches his wife, Marie-Christine, absorbed in the task of dressing. Unconsciously, he is fascinated by the feminine mechanism of these evening activities. He lives in hiding from himself.

"Raphael, my stole!"

He gathers in the whole of her sleeping smile.

(And her children have inherited her hardness! They give me orders. My house has been invaded by a monstrous regiment.)

He hands her the stole with a heavy gesture. The woman shakes back her hair.

(Ah, this anticipation has been aroused in her by a man not myself! Soon, when this mask of harshness has been stripped off, the lover will be taking a face and a body to which I am a stranger. I am not ignorant of the privileges that a lover enjoys. Marie-Christine, why is that brow of yours so pure? That brow belongs to my favorite son, Christopher. That innocence is not your own.)

"Where are you going this evening?"

"I told you. To this party."

"Will you dance again?"

"Isn't life meant to be enjoyed? You're too serious! Always deep in some terrifying meditation! Is it God that's disturbing you?"

"No, it's myself. But it's God too. And the whole world. And you, Marie-Christine. When I was twenty, I lived by rejecting the future. Now I wish I could reject the past and the present—your present, Marie-Christine."

"The future, there is only the future for men." (Marie-Christine refuses to countenance the spark of complicity that has flashed unbidden into her thoughts at his words.) "I have brought children into the world to look after the future."

"Ah, but the disaster, Marie-Christine, the disaster that is about to hurl itself upon us!"

"The end of love is something that everyone has to go through. So don't be afraid. In all the tragedies I perform, I am a woman quite content with the absence of love."

"There was a time when I begged my sister, when I said to her . . ."

"Raphael, that's enough. Will you never grow up?"

"I want to see the snow in my own country again."

"No, I won't go back there, Raphael."

(Yes, I shall see it again. The snow has its roots too deep inside me. You can't understand, Marie-Christine. The snow is an excuse for idleness of mind and body. You belong to an itinerant world. I am part of a country where nature is as solitary as man himself.)

"My gloves, Raphael!"

He hands her the gloves without a glance.

(It is the mingling of love and anguish inside her that makes her body triumphant.)

"Why didn't you come riding yesterday? My horse was so frisky and wild . . ."

"You're splendid when your horse runs away with you, Marie-Christine, your long, boy's body . . ."

"Oh, Raphael, stop it."

"My brother left home when he was sixteen. I shared his revolt. Nicolas died. I escaped. Our days were peopled with ghosts."

"Oh, Raphael, this insane need of yours to talk!"

Then, in a different tone: "It's tomorrow we leave for Goldefein."

"I wanted to burn down the house. 'Why this hatred?' Yance asked me. But I never knew."

"You can leave me, Raphael. There are the children. But perhaps you would learn to love them better if you were away from me."

"I love you, Marie-Christine."

"Don't lie. I'm not the little girl of our youth any more."

(Yes, her eyes are too big, her lips are too sad, and her passions flow like sensuous streams beneath the transparent glaze of her excesses.)

Marie-Christine gazes at the window, head bent. Raphael

is still thinking about his son, Christopher. Then Marie-Christine speaks: "I'm staying in. My party is you. I dressed up like this for you."

"What is going on, Marie-Christine? The fire, do you see?"

"No, I see nothing."

"There is a red glow over the woods."

"I can't see anything."

"The end of the world is still at my heels. I shall die soon."

"You're shaking."

"Marie-Christine, love me so much that the world can't end. Let silence come quickly! Save the angel living in my body! Save the man living in my blood."

"They've brought the horses back in. What are you afraid of now?"

"You will go back to your own country. Alone."

"Yes, tomorrow."

(When I was ten, we used to act out the passion of Christ. We tortured one another for fun, and I was afraid. We beat Christopher, ten-year-old Christopher, down by the bridge. He yelled: "I don't want to be the one who's killed!" We drew lots. "Is it you, Louis? Anthony? Hugh? Answer . . ." I was the head of the gang, and suddenly I thought of Christopher. "The one who's crucified in the books is called Christopher." "No, he's called Christ. Our mother told us. Haven't you got a mother?" Yes, I have a mother, but she's in a tomb. I chose Christopher because he was innocent. We beat him down by the bridge, with our fists, with our feet. We scourged him, but we didn't nail him up by the hands and feet. Christopher, I named my own son Christopher, so that I should remember . . .)

The woman feels no distress. Her body, like her soul, is still half in a dream. She dresses without thinking and goes out into the night. The world is still alive. She was right. One is justified in putting one's confidence in the earth, and in the world's joy. And in the world's wretchedness too. She laughs. The fire that frightened her husband is only a bonfire on the shore. She walks down toward the water.

What Marie-Christine has interrupted is no more than a children's game. She is plunged once again into the gloom of her former convictions.

"Our ghost!"

"It's not a ghost, it's my mother!"

"Christopher!"

The child detaches himself from the wall of faces and outstretched hands. Their magic fire firmly clenched in their fists, the boys all chant:

It is a celebration, a celebration,
This fire will keep the wolves away,
And the lambs are hiding in the waves.

Then the children move off, trampling the fire out with their feet as they go. Marie-Christine takes her son's hand and they too walk away, holding themselves upright, like two triumphant people marching toward the dawn of a new age.

"Tell me, Christopher, tell me . . ."

The child knows well enough what is meant. It is wrong to run away from one's family at night. But this was only the first night. The boy is sleepy.

"Tell me, Christopher . . ."

"We were playing the 'End of the World,' Mother."

They go back in. Tomorrow neither will remember anything of what has passed, and God will begin to die all over again in their hearts.

Retrace your steps, Oh my Life,
You can see well enough that the road is closed.

Anne Hébert

Raphael has left Marie-Christine and come back to his own country. It is the time of winter snows.

Six o'clock in the morning. Raphael is walking through the blizzard's heart. The great white trees are gaping, bending, mingling with one another. Has it finally come? Is this the morning of all destruction? The blizzard wind is already singing the apocalypse.

"Your life, brother, what have you done with your life?"

"I have searched."

The snow is deep. The mountains are entirely veiled in fog at six in the morning. And leaning over the brink of his fallen being, he understands himself without effort, he feels pity for his own defeat.

It is six in the morning and there is no sun.

(I am walking and walking and it is just as it was in my life when I could never find any of the roads.)

It comes into his mind that they might well crucify Christ here, deep in this forest on this barbarous morning: he sees the tree of punishment before him. He stops. He looks at it. The tree has been dead for a long time. Raphael walks toward his own image. The wood of the tree is suffering as his own flesh is: suddenly it is terrible to see himself reflected in this way.

"Marie-Christine, my wife!"

If she doesn't come, this tree will seize hold of him and teach him how to die.

"Goldefein! Goldefein!"

But he has no way of fighting against what has at last overtaken him: the disaster. Better to give oneself of one's own accord.

There is no snow in his clothes. The flesh of the cold rises against his skin, wrapping itself around him like the final mask of things. Raphael lies in the cold of the tree and is silent. Now he will wait. The snows will rise, the snows will come to him.

It is seven o'clock. Day is waning. The blizzard is over and the sun is freeing the two gray arms of the mountain from their bonds. And it is now, as the man lies dead of the cold and the silence, that the fire of morning burns over him without reaching him. And the man's smile is one of uncertain and unremembering tenderness.

The sun has sacrificed a man in order that a tree may bloom.

At eight o'clock, on that same day, the child begins to feel uneasy.

"Mother, I want to go out on the bridge."

"We're catching our train at nine o'clock. You must stay here with your big brothers."

"But, Mother, you can see the snow fall, out on the bridge."

"There is no snow. You've never seen any snow."

(Mother, look at her empty hands. Our nurse is bored. I want to go to a country where there's snow, the way Father did.)

"You ought to be happy, Christopher, a little boy like you who's been to so many places . . ."

"I've never seen the snow."

"Count all the countries on your fingers, Christopher, and tell me how many . . ."

"Eight, Mother."

"No darling, you haven't counted right."

"I want to go out on the bridge."

"You'd forget to come back. You're always forgetting, like your father."

"I want to go and play on the bridge with my friends."

"What was the name of the forest where I broke my ankle riding?"

"Swan Forest, Mother."

"No, that wasn't it, Christopher."

(We played a game on the beach. What is this bad game you're playing in the dark? Mother asked.)

"We're playing the 'End of the World,' Mother."

"Christopher, you're being unreasonable."

"I know, Mummy."

"But what is it you have on your mind?"

"I want to go out on the bridge."

"Very well then, Christopher, you can go and play on the bridge. But don't stay out long."

A clear white light falls across the bridge, catching the little boy unawares. The cold is trembling inside his chest again.

"Do you want to play with us, Christopher?"

Christopher doesn't answer. But he holds up his fists ready to fight. Once more, he is looking at the legs of his enemies. The enemies are strong, and their hands are as huge as the moon.

It all began with the wish to be grown up, just that. Also, the big boys promised him that he would see the snow.

"Come on then!"

The little boy defends himself with the whole strength of his shivering body. But the big boys are still standing there on the bridge, caught in the shifting play of the wan reflections. The nonexistent snow . . .

The little boy is lying on the bridge, and already the big boys with their heavy feet, are trampling on him.

It feels better when the fight is over. Just a little longer and he'll get up again. (For Mother did say nine o'clock.) The snow is falling. (Ah, if only it weren't nine o'clock yet!) And the child touches his forehead, touches the blood there, and feels that this is what it means to die.

THE HOMECOMINGS

"I am crossing the tall cities to be with you again, my love. I am coming now to be yours. Listen to me, Yance, I am coming back . . ."

"Joshua, you are my lover."

"Lisa, you must go now, quickly. What are you doing? What are you suffering for me?"

"I am a woman that you loved."

"There is a woman waiting for me and you are not that woman."

"Joshua, there was the sea . . ."

"Yance will be alone in the big house. Yance is waiting for me. Lisa, goodbye."

"My love."

"I shall hear your step on the stairs. The lamps will have burned a long time for my return. Lisa, why did you come? The paths across the dunes, the salt in your hair, Lisa. But happiness was no longer in those things."

"And the child I want?"

"Lisa, be silent. One kills the child one desires when it is born. I already have a daughter."

"And what am I then?"

"Your face was Yance's face, yet not her face. Yance is waiting for me. She will give me the silence of God."

Lisa, goodbye. Goodbye, my second youth!

Yes, I recognize my town, your paths, our house. Yes, I recognize the men and the women of our town and the footsteps that we have forgotten, from our student days. And I think of Black Island and how you loved me there. I loved you too and did not know it. Yance! Yance! I have learned now how not to live with shadows. I am present at last. I shall love the warmth of your fingers on my cheeks.

The uncompleted lover is returning! Lisa has wept. Yance will weep for joy.

My love stroked my body to sleep with his right hand,
My lover caressed my shoulders as I lay in the sun . . .

Yance, soon I shall see your face. And I will not leave you again.

The woman no longer recognizes the town of her youth. But she can see her house as it shines like a wan sun at the entrance to a valley. Where is the young woman of yesterday who kept vigil over an everlasting darkness? Where is Genevieve?

Dusk is falling. And in that dusk the children's footsteps have lost the rhythm of their past childhood. Yance observes the adolescents that she sees, their legs, their hands like heavy ghosts, their faces masking a cruel and precocious weariness. "Yes, our world has known suffering."

Things wrapped in unawareness before have been stripped of their veils, and the dreamy-eyed little girls of yesterday have been transformed into grown girls and young women bereft of freshness.

In the groups of boys and girls crossing the park, she recognizes the youth of her exile and her own time: ravaged, misunderstood, and guilty children. It comes into her mind that the most atrocious thing that could happen to the world, before the end of time, would be something very like this dismembered generation, a host of young people sent from hell to damn the world. Yes, like a plague they would spread over the land, these children of meaninglessness, and despair would root its insinuating body limb by limb into the earth. These children ask for neither hate nor love. They have been summoned to a task of destruction, as Raphael, her brother, once foresaw. It is the desire for death that keeps alight the sickly glow of genius in their eyes . . .

At the far end of the park lies the waiting house, and the man, yes, surely the privileged lover who will understand her still, the being who will share a full existence with her, a humble integration with life's joy. The woman feels a cold hope inside her. Before reaching the house, she must cross the park, she must undergo the struggle . . . Ah, those shoulders and necks in the darkness! That wall of faces with their scornful mouths! A whole generation stands petrified there to face her, like a frozen wound!

"Greet, it's Greet come back to dance with us. Where have you been these last three years?"

The shoulders and the arms loosen and part. Yance is allowed inside the frozen circle of their dance, surrounded. She feels cold. She thrusts her fists deep into the pockets of her raincoat. (The world's sickness has already begun, Yance thinks, the plague across the earth.)

"Greet, dance with us!"

Unmoving, the woman waits for the game to be over.

"Greet, you've become so beautiful! Tell us what it's like on the other side . . ."

"Where do you mean?"

"On the other side of town of course, Greet!"

"There are men and women forgetting!"

The young man looking at her with those dark eyes of his is tomorrow's murderer. She can tell. (Is it not decreed that the world shall perish by the hand of a child?)

"And you, Greet, have you been loved?"

"Yes," the woman says.

The young man speaks to her gently. "Then you have found the time to love, have you?"

Tomorrow these children will crucify the Christ. They will cover the earth in fire and blood.

The evening is warm. The woman has been set free. She walks on alone.

(I shall find you again, my love. We have suffered. It has been difficult to caress bodies that were not yours. It has been easy loving men who were not you. You are the most absurd of lovers, the most disembodied, the most inhuman in your beauty! I am Yance. I am entering our house. Come close to me. It has been so long. Do not make me wait any more.)

The man does not come.

Emptiness appears there. The man has not come. He will not come. In the miracle of memory, Yance can still feel her child in her womb. But the pain of that is too great, for in that memory she also feels regret for all the children that she has not had.

(He named her Beloved Dream.)

The woman goes through into the study. She switches

on the lamp over the fireplace, as she used to before. The lamp on the piano has been broken. She could read the novels her husband never finished . . . She could wait for Genevieve! (No, I don't want to see that insubstantial, untouched creature, that madwoman who will take up time and our words at the exact point where we left them twenty years ago.)

But Genevieve has come.

"Genevieve, it's me!"

And only then did Yance see those lips relax their thin line, those eyes open to reveal a captive and unexpected understanding.

"Roxane, my child!"

"You know that I'm Yance! Why are you determined not to recognize me?"

Genevieve laid her hands on Yance's shoulders. Suddenly Yance felt herself become very tiny, as though she were once more the little girl who hid in Genevieve's skirts. In those days, Genevieve was real, her face was not simply this expanse of lost and inexpressive features. Genevieve was alive then. She had Nicolas.

"Roxane, what have you done with the baby? What have you done with Nicolas?"

"Genevieve, Genevieve, what have you done with my child? What have you done with Roxane?"

"I remember your saying it one evening: 'I want to kill Nicolas.'"

"Yes, I killed Roxane."

"Who was that man who brought you here? Who was that young man? And what have you done with him?"

"Joshua. His name is Joshua."

"Roxane, I've been waiting for you. You did well to forget the child. The dead do not belong to us. It is for me alone to think about him and bring him back to life."
"Genevieve! Genevieve!"

The young people have left the park. The most absurd of lovers has not come. Yance still listens for his faithful step. Yance has nothing now but her solitary soul to guide her.

And as Joshua walks back into the town with his mad hope deep in his eyes, he recognizes the universe of his youth. He is able to recognize it now, he who has never felt any bond with the world of things. And at dawn, he reaches home . . .

Joshua is beautiful. Beautiful but tragic: the women walking silently through the morning prefer to forget him. They turn away their heads at the sight of that soul. They do not seek to make him smile at them. A soul without a body cannot give itself, or if it does, then it gives itself too incompletely not to be dangerous. Those women have learned many things at their lovers' sides: they know what man's beauty is, man's heart, his instincts and his senses. They have tamed their lover's appetites enough to know how much the soul should be mistrusted. The man who is too pure and innocent repels them. Or else he fascinates them, like a distant glimpse of God's approach in the eyes of desire. And these women, heavy with the passing darkness and rekindled love, walk past Joshua with indifference.

The man is enchanted by the women's grace, the grace of their arms with the hunger and kisses of the night still upon them, the wounded grace in their eyes, and the wretched grace of their blond hair. Joshua is taking humanity into his child's heart at last.

And it is perhaps through these things, because the man has always seemed still-born inside him since birth, until now, that Joshua has come to this experience of a universal existence: he is no longer a body responsible only for itself, he is a flower, a summer breeze, the dusty open road, he is the sky, the bird with motionless wings caught in its high ecstasy, he is a spring. He is unable, at last, to go on not being.

Joshua recognizes the streets of his own town and is filled with a sensation of having been happy, already. There was a woman who held his arm at this spot, the woman who came to wait for him in September, at five o'clock . . .

(At five o'clock. It was at five o'clock that our daughter was born!)

The child had never existed for him then, but this morning she is born at last, with all those humble realities that make up the beginning of a day.

(At five o'clock there was a black lamp near the window, and a bouquet of ferns held in a woman's hands.)

Joshua sees the schools, the university, even the church he attended, all those deserts of his youth . . .

(In the morning there was always a young girl trailing along the boulevard, a little girl from the dance hall.)

And he sees the little, sullied girl as she wanders home from her nighttime horrors. She smiles at him. He smiles back, from somewhere beyond the harm that he was once able to inflict . . .

His house is dancing before him dressed in all the colors of the sun.

Joshua is home.

"Joshua, how I've been waiting for you!"

Already a woman's fingers are closing around the warmth of his neck.

"You are sweet," he says.

The garden room. The scents of the past . . .

"Joshua, don't go to sleep. It's been so long."

"I'm here," he says.

"How I love you."

"There's nothing to be afraid of, not any more!"

The man takes the woman's head between his hands.

"You are so pale!" he says.

Stunned and dizzy, he moves away from the woman and watches her, obscure somehow in her cruel transparency.

"Don't go yet!"

He longs to seek extinction in a death of shadows. But the woman still laments!

"Joshua, my love, it's I, Genevieve!"

☼ ☼

It is summer. Ten o'clock. Another day.

Two delicate hands open the shutters. The mist that has swathed the garden since the coming on of night now billows strangely upward; it flows into the house; it brings the color of the darkness in through the walls and spreads its beauties across the faces straining there to scan the darkening day.

"Joshua, what can you see on the road?"

"It looks like a very young girl."

"Is she coming this way?"

"Yes."

(I was with my wife. At dawn she said to me: "Where are you going, Joshua?" "I want to go out and walk in the mist." And since that time I have never been back.)

Genevieve can see the man weeping, but she is not thinking of him. She stands there, as she always stood, a statue of grief.

Death. Joshua was dead. He had chosen immateriality as one chooses damnation.

"Genevieve!"

(Oh, let her make that gesture, let her speak that word, and let her follow me!)

The Child will return to the House of Shades,
The child will come back in the cool of the dawn.

(Oh, be silent, Genevieve!)

He walks. His only thought is to put that house of death behind him. His body of mist and fog falls away from him of its own accord.

The young woman or the young girl passes him without seeing him. Joshua has forgotten those who are going to die because of him. He does not know that the young girl opening the garden gate is already fated to destroy herself.

Roxane seems to hear her name called: "Beloved Dream," but the man does not halt his steps and has no memory of that dream.

The young woman walks on alone into the house of death. And everything must begin again, as it is beginning again today, as it began again yesterday . . .

EPILOGUE

"Good evening, you are all shining in the rain!"
"It was so cold there. I came before it was dark."
"It has been a long day. Take my hand."
"We are alone forever."

"And now?"
"There was nothing left but a lie."
"And now?"
"There was nothing left between us but time."
"I came. I am here."
"I see you. I thought that your face would still be the same. A lover's face does not change between morning and evening."

"Between morning and evening a man may understand."

"We came to this same wedding when we were twenty."
"I said, quite simply: Goodnight, Joshua."
"And I replied: Goodbye, Yance."
"And it is still midnight."

THREE
TRAVELLERS

Moment One

Allegro Vivace. First movement

Those wonderful hands, still raised in an unresolved pause, were waiting, as in a dream, for the supple swelling of the orchestra's return. Waiting for the moment of harmony. The fingers scarcely quivering above the keyboard: perhaps they were already sliding on the backs of living waves, suspended over the silence of invisible rivers?

So Miguel thought as he sat beside his wife, Montserrat, in that Paris concert hall. He was only one witness of the music among others, a traveler through reality enjoying a sweet moment of rest, this Sunday, this May 3. Miguel loved this Mozart concerto.

It was four o'clock. Miguel was himself moving forward into the decline of the day, a decline as dark as the sun that was shadowing the long, ribbed vaults, at that very moment, in all the cathedrals of France. The night-filled cathedrals that he had gazed at, with Montserrat by his side, on Tuesday and Wednesday.

"This week is going slowly," Montserrat had said as she walked beneath the great flaming and ashen arches. "I'm tired." Miguel had been disturbed because she was breathing so slowly: it had been as painful for him as that morning when she had smiled at him so impatiently, at the foot of the staircase in a great house in Spain. That fixed, sour smile, dark in the shadows. There were moments when Montserrat felt herself brutally clawed by an indefinable feeling of age, and her remedy then was to breathe very fast, believing that this immediately dissipated the flood of boredom or anger rising inside her. Miguel was afraid of mortal passions: Montserrat could betray their presence with a single breath.

"It's Sunday, Miguel, my love."

No, she hadn't spoken. She was listening. She was watching the hands of the young pianist as they wandered in distant, limpid circles that she alone could see. She had sculptured that face, she had sculptured those hands, in stone, in wood . . . Was it on Thursday, Friday, or Saturday? She closed her eyes.

Miguel was tenderly aware that she had closed her eyes so that she would be free to exist only through herself, submissive to the violent night of her being. In this way, Montserrat was able to begin remembering with greater calm.

Montserrat. Montserrat.

He was simply saying her name to sound the depths in which she was living. Then suddenly, ah! to seize that love as it fled away.

Miguel. Miguel.

"Go away from me, Johann."

She had sculptured that face in wood, yes, on Wednesday, on Thursday, and on Friday. She had thrown a veil over those uncertain but splendid features; the gaze, above all, had pierced her with its fugitive and painful grace.

"Go away from me, Johann."

"Johann has to go back to Italy on Sunday, for the Venice Festival. He's expected there. Will you go too, Montserrat?"

"I shall stay in Paris with Miguel."

Known and unknown voices woke in her consciousness. "Tonight I shall sleep much better," Montserrat thought (she was no longer thinking about Johann's hands playing only for her), yes—what a sleep it will be, won't it, Miguel? Like the sleep we slept in Spain, the heavy sleep that left us like naked castaways on a miraculously pale beach."

Johann was experiencing an hour of glory this Sunday afternoon: Miguel had fallen as he tried to attain a similar pinnacle the Sunday before, at the same hour of the day. They would always be separated from one another by a deep gulf of happiness. "Why is it you, Johann, rather than me? Why are you the chosen one?" "Tonight I shall sleep at last," Montserrat thought.

She could recall with perfect clarity the failure that had torn at her husband last Sunday, in the theater, at the first performance of his play. "Perhaps it was then that Miguel lost his faith, rather than on Monday, in the cathedral at Chartres?"

She opened her eyes.

Johann was waiting for the orchestra, his head bent forward over his huge, inanimate hands.

That was how she had quickly drawn his face on an old sketch pad, before daring to mold that brow into the shape of a piece of wood, on Sunday, yes, on Sunday, already the day of Miguel's failure?

Montserrat. Montserrat, Miguel said without looking at her, during the first movement . . .

Sunday . . .

SUNDAY

What was the young poet's purpose in writing this story of uncomprehended angels? Why this Last Judgment? No one knows. What is going on in the mind of this clumsy and disturbing creator who believes that it is the lives of human beings he is conjuring up, even when his characters are continually slipping from his grasp and undergoing sudden metamorphoses into agile and ironic ghosts? How did he create this slow torture drawn from the depths of time, how did he find the immodest strength to make it live outside of himself? Tell me, Miguel, I so want to know.

Those were Johann's thoughts as he sat beside his mistress, Montserrat, in that Paris theater. He liked this play. He could not prevent himself from loving it passionately. But the audience had no wish to experience this fresh torment . . . the soul of Miguel, Miguel, a man unheard of until then. The crowd was tired, it was no longer willing to experience suffering or revolt. Why should they bother to pass judgment on the man who loses his soul, or the man who saves his soul? It was a long time since God had ceased to exist for all these minds. And all alone, a young man named Miguel went on with his struggle against the shadows, slipping silently through the darkness of the actors' world—behind the mute flats, slave and master of an absolute inspiration that he watched spreading around him like the lament of some ingenious beast—recognizing without a moment's respite the cry of his own freshly delivered heart in every line, in every breath, beneath the tombstone of every silence, twisted on the universal masks of his characters.

And yet, as Miguel was well aware—this tragedy of his was merely an error. He was watching an error made flesh. Now he would have the courage to wait for the noble failure of this poem he had made, a poem as long and as short as life. He was no longer afraid of anything.

It was four o'clock. Johann was moving forward into the decline of the day, as deeply shadowed as the body he had held fast through the night, and whose wild and flickering glow was still alive in him even now.

"This week is going by too fast," Montserrat had said as she stroked his hair.

"Don't you love your husband?"

"Yes, I love him. I love him violently. But you must go away from me. You are my misfortune, your face has been pursuing me since I was born, I shall never resist you."

"There is so much I didn't know," the man answered.

"You were still a very young man, not yet sixteen. I saw you play a Mozart concerto in Vienna. I fell in love with you for eternity."

"That year (*it was just after a war and I was trying to make an abstraction of those years*) I played the same concerto in Austria. And I met young musicians who had come from all the countries in the world, and conductors, and composers. Among all these people I met, there was a young woman who has since become my wife."

"Why didn't she come to Paris with you?"

"She is expecting our second child."

"We mustn't talk any more," the woman said.

The first act was still not over. Miguel was thirsting for silence. When would it be over?

Montserrat. Johann. The two people he loved most on earth. He could see them. They were born to be there, now, today, in order to be gazed at by the innocent, banished soul of Miguel: harsh, victorious, bruised. Johann. Montserrat. They were beginning to live at the very moment when Miguel was entering his death agony. Why had she introduced him to Johann, on Saturday, why had she invited Johann to drink champagne with them on Saturday, and why that Saturday?

Darling, for a long time now I've been wanting you to meet a man you'll like very much. It's not right that you should be alone.

"I'm not alone. I live with you."

He had seen him for the first time on Saturday, when Montserrat was talking about making a bust of him. Johann Van Smeeden. Miguel despised the way his memory would not let anything die. Everything was still happening on the flamelit stage before him. Montserrat bringing her glass to her lips with a softly molded gesture that folded her arm around Johann's silhouette; this invisible embrace was perceived only by Miguel, bound to all that was happening elsewhere. Montserrat was tipping back her head and drinking slowly, showing her teeth. Her new love had transformed her into a woman streaming with a joy that took its source in a new body.

"I feel wretched, Johann. You oughtn't to leave on Sunday. But perhaps you will find the rest you need in Venice?"

"I expect to find more than rest."

"Don't tell me what. I don't want to know."

"There will be a great many friends waiting for me there. Why shouldn't you be one of them?"

"That's impossible. Miguel wants to go back to Spain on

Sunday. We haven't been back to Spain since . . . How long is it, Miguel?"

"A very long time," Miguel said.

"No, no, we won't let you go."

She gave a bored laugh. Miguel watched her laughing, her right hand pressed against her lips. No. She was stifling a forbidden word, a word of amazement. Montserrat never laughed out of boredom. Miguel watched himself moving toward Montserrat. "Are you thirsty, Montserrat?" "A little, Miguel."

He watched himself fill the stemmed glass, then hold it out toward Montserrat's gloved hand. She was wearing a velvet dress with its folds stretched tight over the angle of her knees. Her smooth calves were the color of fruit.

"Miguel never drinks. Miguel works very hard. I always have to remind him that it's past midnight. If that's what Miguel wants, then we shall go back to Spain."

The invisible embrace was broken off by a glance from Johann.

"No, go away from me."

"You know very well that I have to go back, and this Sunday, too."

At this point, the motionless lovers had moved apart. Johann began to talk about spring in Paris, about the strange freshness that young girls in Paris have.

"There is an omnipotent quality of hope in the eyes of the young girls," Johann said.

"What sort of hope do you mean?"

"You could never see it," Johann said, his face overcast.

"Yet my husband knows a great deal about such things, and he tells me about them as soon as he sees them," Montserrat answered.

"I am unhappy in your presence," Johann said. "I haven't the power to understand you, and you know it."

Montserrat bowed her head and smiled. "But we are not in a state of distress."

Her hand was trembling. She was forgetting to drink her champagne. Her knees were trembling, almost imperceptibly. Miguel stroked her shoulder with a compassionate hand. "It's nothing," he said in a low voice. "Don't let it upset you." She summoned fresh strength, holding herself upright at the center of her swaying and uncertain being. "This young man is trying to disturb us."

"You are right, Montserrat."

"We have never been sad," Montserrat went on, as though trying to console a child (*and the child was that poor soul imprisoned inside who was never to be brought into the world*), "have we, Miguel?"

"No, never," Miguel answered.

At that point, Miguel had employed surprise tactics to alter the course of their conversation.

"How do you set about playing a concerto?" he asked. "It's a thing that's always been wholly mysterious to me . . ."

"Don't lie," Montserrat broke in (*her voice was no longer trembling, her voice was more serene*). "We're both of us too passionate, you know. Miguel won't learn how to control himself. Think how he coped with the astonishingly complex machinery of a theatrical production. I was able to watch it all very closely at the dress rehearsal. I was dumfounded. He is extraordinary but yet he knows nothing. He is fantastic sometimes," Montserrat said (*slowly, slowly, speaking only for Johann's benefit now: Miguel had moved away for a moment to close the blinds*). "He doesn't know anything because he allows himself to be lacerated by everything that moves him. I don't know him very well. Don't listen to me like that, Johann. You'll be able to discover more about my husband for yourself. But you will see, as I did when he used to build those castles made of waves when we were in Spain, you will see that everything he builds, everything he writes is constantly threatened with collapse like a palace made of sand."

"I pity him with all my soul," Johann said.

"He would like to be able to pity you, too," Montserrat said.

She took Johann's hand, she lowered her voice, she murmured: "Ah! what delight you feel at being one of the immortals."

"No, please try to understand . . ."

Miguel was walking toward them. They fell silent. Miguel came and sat down beside Montserrat.

"I suddenly felt hot," he said.

"We must all learn to live with the flames that rise in us at every moment," Montserrat said.

Then she fell silent.

This silence lay like a great weight on Miguel as he tried unsuccessfully to will the first act of his tragedy to a close. There was a man—himself—standing out there alone and talking to the audience.

Johann and Montserrat seemed to be only half listening. Together, they made up a single, riveting face.

"Yes, it was on Saturday that I saw you for the first time, Johann. I can't say what it was I felt then. My wife loved you. You had made love to her during the night. But you stood there before me, without anger and without hate, as I stood before you. Montserrat was radiant with your innocence. You were conscious of not hiding your love for Montserrat in any way from me, just as I was not hiding my love for her from you. We were equally matched adversaries. Why did you tear at me at that moment, just when I was seeing you for the first time?"

"Make him go away from me."

Montserrat was carving your face out of the wood. And there you were, a little distant from everything, and above all from yourself, without interest in those gestures that were making you into a mere model, or rather into a victim—I no longer know which: those gestures of Montserrat's that were already throwing bonds around you . . . You were the prisoner of an unknown twilight. Montserrat must have felt love for you, else how could she have desired to imprison her own being thus in that perishable model? But were you perishable? Are you now? I could sense the chaste burden of immortality weighing down your head.

And then I was drawn toward you, as lightning is by silence, like the night when it can no longer hold back from the day declining to its goal, not as a woman is drawn by her lover, but more as the abyss, in a region higher even than death, is sucked upward by an angelic strength. You were the angel of light, the tempting angel who had come for my salvation or my perdition, you were the angel.

Tirelessly, silently, miraculously, my wife's hands were taming your features; but were they capturing that inner light, that untamable transparency? Montserrat composed your face at the expense of her own shadows. "I've never seen anyone as still as you before, Johann," she said with a smile. I measured the abysses opening within her by sounding the depths of that breathing, so near to regret, to remorse, to the most burning disquiet. How could I ignore the way she leaned over to peer down into her despair?

"Don't you ever smile, then, Johann?"

"It will be possible to smile one day without destroying everything around one, don't you think so too?"

"No," Montserrat said.

In front of her sculpture, she was more and more un-yielding. In front of the man, she was prepared to bow.

"Talk to us, talk to me," I said . . .

No, I wouldn't have dared to ask it of you.

We had been driven from paradise.

"It's strange," Montserrat was saying. "Miguel believes a great deal in God, but will he still believe in him tomorrow and later on?"

You were indifferent, Johann. It was the indifference that perhaps exists at the heart of a love that must remain inaccessible. Your piercing and frighteningly gentle presence conjured up for me the vision of a world without a name, of a hope whose meaning I had already lost. The angel of light that suddenly opens the oceans of the supernatural to our gaze must bear a heavy burden of guilt. My angel was inhuman.

"No, Johann, be quiet," Montserrat said. "Be quiet, be quiet, will you! I must be left in peace if I'm to work. No young man has ever given me as much trouble as you. And yet I've been moved by a great many faces before yours. You're only another man among many, after all. But there are days when life takes on a certain strangeness. Everything is changed into something else. Don't you think so?"

"Yes," Johann answered, without lowering his eyes. "But the life I lead is a very simple one, you know. Most of the time I am in Vienna with my wife and our child. So far away from music I feel unworthy to be its intimate interpreter. I know of no other life as narrow as mine," he added.

An hour later, when Montserrat seemed to be showing signs of fatigue and of wanting to be alone (*I always recognize the moment when this solitude becomes a matter of urgent necessity for her*), I asked you to come through with me to the studio so that you could look at her work.

"The Temptation." That was the first of her works that we saw together. And to me that sculpture seemed an embodiment of Johann's presence, a searing revelation at the meeting point of our two lives.

" 'The Temptation,' " Johann said. "Why is that young man allowing himself to be made drunk by shadows? It is the darkness to which he is reaching out his arms, isn't it?"

"No," I answered. "He is surrounded by light."

"There is terror in his face: he doesn't know where he is going," Johann said.

"No, his eyes are lucid: his eyes already know everything that lies ahead," I answered.

"Who is this youth possessed by the devil?"

"By the devil? He is not a youth, nor yet a man, but something quite different. How could such a race of beings be possessed by the devil? And does Satan exist?"

"I believe that your wife could not prevent herself, in this work—from bringing the devil into existence," Johann said.

"The Ghosts" was the next work.

"I see souls," Johann said, "more pure souls. Yet a soul can also be a body. Here, I see bodies advancing into the darkness, souls full of wisdom and yet without hope," Johann said. "Bodies without number."

"Yes, without number. Montserrat says that she saw them walking through the night. I wasn't with her. I knew nothing about it all."

"Why do some of the souls have such very young bodies? That one there is a child."

"I had never noticed that before . . ." I said.

"Young Girl in Sleep."

It was simply the head of a little girl. Perhaps Montserrat herself, as a child . . .

"Is she dead?" Johann asked.

"We have no way of telling," I said.

"She is asleep in the curve of a dream," Johann said. "I love that straight neck lighting up . . ."

"And the eyes?"

"Let's not say anything about the eyes," Johann said.

Montserrat came into the room. She came over and took my arm.

"Why did you leave me alone? I went off to sleep."

"You drank too much champagne."

"I have the feeling that I've been raised from the dead," Montserrat said. "It's a comforting feeling."

She lowered her eyes as she stopped in front of the little girl's head.

"That's enough, Johann. Don't try to understand it. Have pity on me."

Then, turning to me: "Why did you do this, Miguel? You know I don't like showing people the things I've made."

"They are all so dense and disturbing," Johann said.

"There is nothing there but life," Montserrat said. "And

my own carries so little weight. Come," she said, "come, my friends."

This time she seized hold of Johann's arm as well as mine. She walked out of the studio between us, so light that she seemed to float in the air.

Montserrat and Johann were still listening. The first act was over. And Miguel was silent.

Intermission

"We'd better go and talk to Miguel, reassure him—he's in hiding because he's in pain."

"No, don't go," Johann said. "You've been crying, and he'll notice it. Let's wait. There's still the second act to come. Who knows? Perhaps Miguel will find peace after all."

"That's strange," Montserrat said. "People are staying in their seats."

"Let's go out for a moment," Johann said. "The night in Paris is so bright; I want to go out and look at it with you."

Johann put his arm around Montserrat and held her against his shoulder. His tall, slender body seemed to raise Montserrat from the ground as they walked. She was drifting with him like a dead leaf. She who had carried everything before her until yesterday.

"It's raining," Montserrat said. "That will do me so much good. It has been raining in Paris for forty days and forty nights. But the fire has not stopped burning for a single moment inside Miguel and me. This unending stifling heat . . ." she added, bending her head.

"The head of the little girl," Johann exclaimed. "I can see it now. The child isn't dead . . ."

A little while before he spoke, they had begun to embrace. The embrace now reached its conclusion in a springtime storm. Johann kissed Montserrat and held her tight in his arms against the wall.

"What do you want to do to me?" she asked. (*The whirlwind raged through her grave eyes like a charging courser.*) "Yes, you must go away from me. You must go away from me."

"Come with me as far as Notre Dame."

"No," Montserrat said. "We must go back to the theater. Miguel is expecting us to be there. He's all alone."

He allowed her the little void of freedom that follows a blind embrace.

"No, don't let me go," she said.

He pulled her against him again.

"I don't know what goes on in your heart. That's the greatest pain I have to bear."

The rain was running down Johann's eyelids, coursing down to his deserted mouth.

"Oh, my bronze idol," Montserrat cried through her laughter. "How absurd it is! My sun god, molded out of light. I worship you."

The rain was glistening on Montserrat's cheeks like waterdrops making flames spurt up from embers. And the beauty of those reviving embers possessed the same clarity as certain shadowy objects when they are suddenly flooded with bright sunlight.

"There are many storms still to come," Johann told her, "but you will never perish."

"I know," Montserrat answered. "I am happy that Miguel exists too."

They were on their way back to the theater now. The oasis behind them had softened Montserrat's laughter.

"You laugh so well and so badly," Johann said.

"You were so much with me down on the quay that I forgot to look at the Seine."

"You also forgot to look at the people running to take shelter from the rain, the people of Paris, the women, the children."

"Forgive me," she said. "I couldn't see anything but you. I couldn't hear anything but you. And I even almost forgot Miguel waiting for us in the theater."

"They have thrown themselves in the Seine," Johann said.

"Who do you mean?" she asked.

"What are you saying? I can't hear you."

"Yes, there have always been wrecks floating in the Seine," Montserrat said.

"Let's walk quicker," Johann said.

"But I'm running now," Montserrat said.

"We must be back in time."

"I've run so far," Montserrat said.

"We must be back in time. But it's too late already," Johann said. "Come on."

Montserrat's waist was curving to the pressure of his hand like an animal yielding itself to the caress of its executioner.

"No, you mustn't think of me as your enemy!"

"Then you think the devil has the misfortune of existing too?" Montserrat cried.

(*But she knew what was happening, knew that she was denying all she had lived through until this moment, for the sake of that hand on her waist holding her over the void; she was savoring its searing touch with terror: and the courser was still hurtling across the peaceful field of her gaze.*)

But it's not he who is the seducer—it's I. Yes, I. I asked you to become my lover. I had never been unfaithful to my husband. It hasn't changed the love I have for him in any way. Devil, she said (*so low that Johann could no longer tell if he was hearing words or sobs*), and not only the demon of unfaithfulness, but that other too, the demon who tries to make you believe that it was God who created him, that he is the Son of God more than I am a daughter of the earth and Miguel's wife. Darling, just be a man, nothing more than a man, I beg of you: only a few more nights with me and you will take on flesh like every living being that has its place in the world.

"Quiet," Johann said, "The stage is lit up. Follow me."

"The first time I saw you, in Vienna, I understood at last who you were. That young pianist with the wild and candid eyes . . ."

"The second act has begun," Johann said.

While they returned to their memories (*though it had only been going on for a short time in fact, already the earth had grown much older and men had continued dying every second, faithfully, punctually, so that Miguel's and Montserrat's thoughts, on this May Sunday, might emerge victorious and dictate their movement to the planets, before the rest, before the Seventh Day of the Creation now approaching*). While Johann's hands, with equal fidelity, were also bestowing life. The second movement of the concerto had begun. Andantino.

As she watched him come into the brown room (*she had lit several lamps, but they were burning low and going out, one after the other, yellow or pink, then brown like Montserrat's own hair, so that she could no longer be sure of what exact color the ecstasy was made; the scented Paris evening, like a damp bird rising from the street after a storm, was flowing in through the swinging shutters*)—she sensed with an ecstatic joy that he was rushing into her room like a propitious wind driving a season of drought before it—tragic like the wind, yes, and wild in his progress as only the wind can be, he was coming to her.

"Montserrat? Montserrat? Why you? Why you, my love?"

"Perhaps if you tell me, then I shall know."

She did not get up. Lying on the bed, her arms outspread and her feet bound together by the darkness, she waited for that face and for those eyes. Slowly, then, he kneeled above her and waited too.

"Where am I?" she asked.

"The rain in Paris is so violent," Johann said. "Can you hear me?"

"No," Montserrat said.

"We had this same great deluge in Vienna a month ago." She let her head fall back.

"Don't you sometimes wear white dresses?"

"When I was a little girl, they used to give me white shoes. Miguel used to run with me through the sand and the snow. One day he touched a thorn against my finger. The blood ran down into my open hand. That was how I was engaged to him. We became engaged to one another often, in the brambles, in summer, in the winter, but most of all in summer. I shall be engaged to him again too. I love him."

"Yes," Johann said, "you love him."

"That was always inevitable."

"Under your green dress, under your blue or green dress (*Montserrat laughed tenderly; he was still unable to tell, still mistaken as he leaned over that body that was being yielded up to him more than ever, even though he had never taken it till now*).

"My dress is red," Montserrat said.

"Under your red dress, what color is your body, tonight?"

He undressed her. He pulled down her arms against her sides.

"Don't stretch your arms out to infinity. Make yourself into one line, with your soul running through the center, like those souls I was looking at earlier."

"They were moving forward into the night, and they were numberless, more numberless than the stars," Montserrat said. "That is my husband's poem."

She sighed.

"How naked I am," she said. "Have I just been born? Are you my judge?"

"We are together," Johann said. "And your darkness is your beauty. Your body is in revolt." ("Yes, it is in revolt against all things that die," Montserrat thought.)

The darkness became complete and Montserrat allowed her feet and her hands to be untied.

She had just dressed herself again and was lying stretched out beside Johann: the man asleep was dearer to her than even the sleep itself, so great had been her desire to know this man and this sleep that was irresistibly making him more human still.

"I always knew you were only a man. I am satisfied now that I know he exists inside you, that man. Miguel may believe in God and in your existence too, Johann, but I am safe now both from God and from you. I shall go on searching to find out who you are so that I can become the most human of quarries when I am with you. I am not being unfaithful to Miguel with Satan. I am being unfaithful to him with a man. And you are perhaps no more than Johann Van Smeeden, a musician I met once in Vienna who has now come to Paris to play a Mozart concerto. But whoever you may be, you are a temptation to me and you have been hunting me down since the day I was born."

Johann took Montserrat's hand.

"Who did that?" he asked. "Who made your finger bleed? What thorn has pierced it, and for what still boyish fiancé?"

"Sleep a little longer," Montserrat said. "I was thinking, I think, and I was biting my finger without being aware of it; it was the point of a tooth that pierced my finger. So you can go on sleeping, Johann. I am thinking of Everything."

Montserrat walked into Miguel's room and said: "It's dawn, Miguel; no more time for sleep until the dress rehearsal is over. I promised I would come and wake you. Here I am. What is it that's troubling you?"

"There is an angel in the house," Miguel said.

"Is it really an angel?" Montserrat said.

She raised her husband's head.

"Darling, we are still young, and perhaps there are new times still ahead for us, days even better and sweeter than those of our childhood together in Spain. Keep awake, keep awake, who can tell what will happen?"

"Is it still raining."

"You know I never wear a blue dress when it's raining, Miguel."

"Your dress is green," Miguel told her with a laugh. "You always get it wrong."

"Yes, it's raining, Miguel."

She was in a hurry; she was trying to forget.

"How shadowy you are, Miguel, and oh, how much I want you! Yes, we'll go wherever you want."

But how could we go back to Spain again? (She had told Johann about the shoes she had lost. Now she remembered that suddenly.) Let's go to Rome, my love. Or to Greece, the way we used to before. Ah! Why do you always write these great agonies?

Was that all, then? Was the tragedy over? Was there no more to it than that? The audience remained in their seats. Ironic, untouched by even the least astonishment, they stayed seated in their darkened rows: monotonous ranks of enemies in whom anger and hatred could no longer rouse interest or expectations.

The curtain fell. Deep inside himself, Miguel heard a cry ring out. He grew somber.

There had been no resurrection. He had been wrong. After the tragedy, after his patient unraveling of scenes and words, there was nothing left but that one poor cry. One cry that he alone could recognize, since he had heard it on the day that he was born.

"Get up, Montserrat. Go to him. Get up, Montserrat. He needs you. Run and find him."

"That would be madness," Montserrat said. "I won't. Do

you think I shall be able to bear the knowledge of his suffering? I love Miguel."

"You must be with him at this moment," Johann begged.

But Montserrat huddled herself down in her seat and would not get up.

MONDAY

In the train taking them to Chartres, Miguel and Montserrat were fleeing from the all-devouring rain in Paris. From time to time, as it was abruptly plunged into the dawn light, Miguel's face would drink in the gold from a sudden rift that bathed his brow in sadness. Flooded with a brief inner peace, he drew away from Montserrat's hand as it sought his wrist.

"What is there to complain of, Miguel? We are together. We shall visit paradise. Then we shall leave it again. They promised us so much in Spain, once upon a time, before we were grown up, before the age of things, long ago. The age of the first pain that is aware of itself. Why have I forgotten all they promised us as we were born? I wanted to be a creature of the earth, of life, quite simply. And what is there for you to complain of, Miguel?" (Her voice was becoming as urgent and warm as the voice of love.) "We have been all around the world together, we have made our quest for what we shall never find. I might have been alone, and so might you. But there you are, and I am with you. The city of Paris was beautiful in our eyes when we were twenty. Because we loved one another. Why are you so ungrateful toward us? Yes, toward us."

Miguel smiled at Montserrat and said, as if in a dream: "When I was in Rome and you weren't with me, what pain it was; you will never know at which moment it was I thought about you, or in which Roman street or garden. Beside which fountain. The sun I saw for you there will never come again; you will never see it with me."

"Ah, Miguel! Do you think that I don't know all that?" Montserrat said.

"No, you don't. Love knows nothing," Miguel said.

"Are all these people coming with us to Chartres?" Miguel asked.

Montserrat answered absentmindedly: "Miguel, I've never known anyone as blind as you are!"

"I think I know you," the young girl said. "Didn't I meet you both last October, in Vienna?"

"Perhaps," Montserrat replied.

"What is your name?" Miguel asked.

"Vinca," the young girl said, "Vinca Van Smeeden. My fiancé will be back in a few moments and I'll introduce him to you. But you know him already. He has gone along to the other compartments to talk to the young people. We are giving a concert this evening, in Chartres. These young people who are making such a noise all around us" (*Montserrat trembled suddenly; until then she hadn't heard a sound*) "are the members of the orchestra. My fiancé selected these musicians from all the four corners of the earth. They are still too young to be perfect players; but my fiancé, who conducts them, has a great deal of confidence in their ability."

Montserrat had already borne the burden of these words before—she could not tell at what exact moment, on what exact day, but she was filled with the certainty of her own foreknowledge.

"And you?" Miguel asked.

"I'm a pianist," the young girl said. "I'm to be the soloist in our Mozart concerto tonight . . ."

She crossed her hands on her knees.

"You seem to be very calm," Montserrat said. "I'm sure everything will go very well for you this evening."

"The orchestra has been well received in Rome," the girl went on. "And in Greece, this summer. Soon we'll be going to Venice."

"To Venice," Miguel said. "It's a city that people are always telling us about, but we are not expecting to go there, my wife and I."

"Jean, do you remember our friends from Vienna?"

"I saw madame for the first time in Austria," the young man said.

He was standing quite still in front of his fiancée, and looking at her in secret while Miguel struggled against his thoughts.

"Come now, Miguel," Montserrat said. "After all, why shouldn't they look like one another? There are several of them living on this earth. They are a race, Miguel, a race that flames with an excessive ardor!"

The young man came and sat down near the girl. Along the narrow corridors of the train, the young musicians were leaning out of the open windows. They had the lightness of doves hovering above a seascape.

Montserrat was going out to meet Miguel's pain: "He says he doesn't believe in God, he says he has lost his belief, but he has perhaps discovered another God . . . the last god of all, the one that exists only for a single moment, for the brief instant of death, the god of the imagination. Take courage, Miguel . . ."

Chartres cathedral was appearing in outline through the mist. "Jean, how bright the sun is on the stone! Jean."

"Tell me about this sun," Miguel said.

But the young man did not answer. The young people were laughing, and their laughter penetrated even into the indifferent ears of Montserrat.

CHARTRES

"This Andantino," Miguel was thinking . . . "Johann plays the world and time, and the infinite swims up through those harmonious gulfs. And the infinite is nothing else, finally, but unfettered joy. Johann knows the secret of the human adventure at last! He knows everything that I do not know, and that I shall never know."

Montserrat. Montserrat.

Sitting there just as he is by her side, she knows that he is seeking for her through the heart of the world.

Montserrat. Montserrat.

We saw the ages writ on every stone, on every door, on every steeple,

It came into the nave through one of those eternal gates,

And suddenly, it vanished.

How did it happen? We could not find out.

Miguel. Miguel.

There was a woman standing at the threshold of the highest door.

She was with child without ever having been a mother, a humble and wounded shape of Innocence.

(An anonymous hand once drew her heart out from the bark of all the trees in France, the setting sun had often set it aflame, but that heart was beating still, a heart forever vulnerable and kind.)

Our-Lady-Beneath-the-Earth,

I lost her at Our-Lady-Beneath-the-Earth,

In a darkened chapel where the fog had followed me. Miguel. Miguel.

"The Virgin is holding her child on her knees—Virgin before she has given birth. Would you like to have a child, Montserrat?"

"No."

"Why not, Montserrat?"

"Without wishing it so, my body will always remain intact."

"And chaste?"

"Yes."

I am walking through the fog, what do you expect?

What do you expect, Miguel?

I am thirsty, here at the Puits des Saints-Forts,

He was thirsty

Peoples now dead have come to drink at this holy well

And you, Miguel?

I'm thirsty.

They flocked here in crowds in the eleventh century, they wanted to cure the wound of humanity.

One drop of this holy water, Miguel

I have been thirsty since yesterday, since you have begun to exist before yourself and after yourself, Montserrat

They flocked here in crowds in the eleventh century, they wanted to cure the dream of humanity

They came, and I am still thirsty. Why?

To the East they built a cathedral, and then another one still,

To protect the first, the ramparts of darkness rose
A long while ago
I am listening to you, Miguel. I can hear you. But the fc ʒ
is hiding
Your beloved face from me.
To the East they built a land of glory.
"You know that on August 5, 962, the fire of dawn . . ."
"No, on September 7 or 8, 1020 . . ."
"And again, soon after, on May 3."
Clothed in spume and in the streaming void
He passed through two long galleries that ran parallel
One to the North, one toward the South
He fled away beneath the arches
Miguel. Miguel.
"And look at that steeple keeping watch over our solitude!"
In the half shadow beneath the steeples
Miguel still walked on, without knowing that the immense statues
Imprisoned against the doors were assuring him of their mysterious presences
He entered into the temple
They watched him do so, like sisters from another age
Their marble eyes, perhaps, filled with nostalgic thoughts
Yet reflecting nothing
They were the captives of their own respect.
On each door, the word, the triumphant word of a sculpture
The Son of God ascending into heaven
Listen, Miguel. See, Miguel.
But he did not look

An old man from the Apocalypse, his face, woe is me
I shall never forget it,
The terrible guardian of the twilight,
 But Miguel wasn't looking. He was walking a long way
away from me.

"Up in the vaulting," Miguel said. "Angels, still more
angels!"

"But they too have to exist, Miguel."

"The life of the Saviour unfolding across the stained-
glass windows, the most misunderstood Passion of all."

"What is in your mind, Miguel? Is it possible for me to
know?"

"No," Miguel replied. "Too late."

Then I noticed a row of horses
Docile because they had just said goodbye to life
When I came upon him again
Miguel was lying on a stone tomb and the fog was gone
The new sun was streaming across his feet and his hands
As though it were that day's blood, even though it had
still not confessed to the great hurt it had suffered.

"How warm it feels, how good it feels," Miguel said.

Handsome sleeper lying there, who am I, can you tell?
No woman knew him as I did
No woman knew less of him than I,

(And then I remembered the sculpture I had finished in
Paris a few days before. "The young man's hope in a
Dream." Miguel was its soul. I was seeing that now. The
arm linked with a mysterious form, the abstract offering of
the smile . . .)

"Come closer," Miguel said. "Tell me, where have you
been?"

"In the crypt," Montserrat said.

Montserrat took off her shoes and walked nearer to him in her bare feet. Simple and majestic, she moved toward him like a curving rope sinking toward the water.

"Montserrat," the voice said, "where were you?"

"I remember our childhood as I look at that madonna. She is always alone beneath her black tears. Like those times long ago."

"What is it you mean?"

"Nothing," Montserrat said.

"Come here," Miguel said.

I stretched myself out beside him and put my arms around him, there, on the stone tomb, below the cathedral of Chartres.

Who knows? Was it a morning in April, a morning in May, or a morning in December? "Tell me, my love, I want to learn the answer from you."

For he taught me everything when we were children: how to love the bunch of grapes brimming over the edge of the basket, how to love the shadow traced on the ground beneath our feet, beneath our sandals as we ran, how to jump off a horse without being afraid of falling. We used to hurtle right off into space, he and I.

I love you. I shall love you.

Speak again.

"One man loves you, and that man is I. Silence within, Montserrat!"

And space was a rose.

We walked through the scents of summer, he and I

The heavy winter rain could not wet us through our blue capes.

"Teach me how to live."

"I am afraid of being weak," Montserrat said. "I am afraid of having grown very old."

"It is life itself that is being made as you go on loving me."

"Yes, life itself. After all, I am not yet as tired as I shall be tomorrow."

"Be silent within, Montserrat. I am searching for you in the depths of the earth."

"It is life itself being made as you go on loving me."

"Yes, life itself. After all, I am only a little bruised."

"You see?" Miguel said. "I am still here."

"Yes, but you aren't the same now," Montserrat answered cruelly.

(*Bewildered, he gazed into the black innocence of her changing eyes*)

"I shall go on loving other men in you; there are thousands still to come."

"Yes, you will go on loving other men in me till the end of the world," Miguel said, "if you are a faithful wife."

"Perhaps I am a faithful wife," Montserrat said.

Little by little, they themselves became the color of the stones they lay on, slim sculptures carved out of springtime beneath the blazing sky.

MONDAY — NIGHT . . .

"Dear soul,"

(*She shivered, and remembered that it was her desire to be no more for him than an illusory but enchanted body— the outward and glittering show of a high, proud passion*) *I* have been working all day with my friends in a damp rehearsal room at the Opéra.

The damp was coming in from Paris flooded, refreshed, and rising from the damp was a fog that crawled around me like a wounded animal.

It was then that I thought of you, Montserrat, the only love of this most precious moment perpetually threatened with an end. I was working on a Beethoven concerto (the fourth) and I can still hear it inside me now, together with the memory of my thoughts of you. How I should like to be your husband so that I could pass on to you the too swiftly changing impressions of that music!

What have you been doing today, Montserrat? Even while you seem the most independent person on earth, I am still afraid that you are too tender a slave. That is why I could never wish to hinder your innocent love of life and death. Go on loving death, Montserrat, since death can never do you harm. (*It contains Miguel's dark felicity.*)

Do you remember the Rondo Vivace? How it is built like a cathedral? The precise voice of the orchestra casting a halo of joy around the silence of each stone, around the slumbering agony of every arching door . . . And suddenly I saw Montserrat as she ran past through the fog, and I lost her.

(*The stones, the silence of each stone: my hand raised above the keys, my whole self waiting in tragic and frozen impotence, forced to go on waiting and waiting. Then, the wild lament of the other instruments wailing into life, among them the song of a violin, chaste as the voice of a child, and I receive the knowledge, abundant and tinged with anguish, that my hands have at last dared to resume their contact with the supernatural.*)

Montserrat. Montserrat.

I saw a great host of colored windows—each one reflecting the color of your gray eyes, and yet, from those darkened windows emanated, all the same, a glow obedient to their tinted substance and the lights: the pillars and the vaulting appeared infinitely deep and infinitely high, so as to lose you better, O Montserrat. . .

The confessors, the immense prophets frozen in eternal impassiveness inside their dream cathedral, watched the passing of a silhouette, your silhouette, one fleeting instant . . .

Then, a stone tomb. And I saw your hand as it pressed another hand, a hand without a hint of succor in it.

O Montserrat.

That is how you were in my heart—all through that Rondo Vivace.

I understood that you had already told me goodbye.

"What are you doing?"

"Reading a letter, Miguel. One from somewhere else."

And you, Miguel, where were you?

"I was listening to a Beethoven concerto."

"You're tired of this day we're spending in Chartres, aren't you?"

"How can I explain to you everything I've understood and everything I've lost in a single day, Montserrat?"

"I know, Miguel. Don't say any more."

"Where are you going, Montserrat? Why do you have your raincoat on? Can't I go with you?"

"Rest, Miguel. I only want to walk as far as the Opéra Then I'll come back when it's dark and go to sleep with you."

"Must we always be saying goodbye then, Montserrat?"

"Yes."

Andantino. A long, contrasting movement. Play, Johann.

The planets spring to life . . . Play, Johann. Everything is immortal and nothing that was will ever be forgotten.

Those wonderful hands, raised still in an unresolved pause, were waiting for the supple swelling of the orchestra's return. Waiting for the moment of harmony. The fingers scarcely quivering above the keyboard: perhaps already sliding across the backs of living waves, poised, in the silence of unseen rivers, between life and death . . .

So Montserrat thought as she sat beside her husband, Miguel, in the Paris concert hall on the third day of May, while the moments in their monstrous course flowed by.

TUESDAY — BOURGES

In Bourges, Montserrat, I lost you in Bourges as you burned with white heat

As on that morning of December 31, 1506, Montserrat

(And who knows, Montserrat, in what century, in what month we were, for I am certain of nothing, except of you when our embrace strips you naked of all words, when love binds us together, and then, at last, you remain what you are)

When the North Tower of the cathedral collapsed

Dragging the vaulting and the great door down in its fall

So the entire cathedral collapsed

Dragging with it your body and mine

And for hours we lay apart.

"Tell me what you were thinking about, Miguel. But I know. In the middle of the sixteenth century. There were five doors here covered with innumerable sculptures as trees are peopled with flocks of birds. First, there was . . ."

Miguel was looking at her. He had never looked at her before in this way. Yes, go on, speak some more, Montserrat. She was disturbed by his look and covered her eyes with the back of her right hand. Thus, sheltering behind an imperceptible veil of pain, she thought about him. He could see her brown eyelashes shining.

"First of all, against the eighth pillar of the great nave there were sculptures representing the scenes of the Passion, and as a screen for the choir . . ."

"No," Miguel said, "that wasn't it."

"And the angels, and the six brass columns."

"That's not what you're thinking about," Miguel said.

I said to her then: "Tell me what you have chosen,
     The flames or me."

For the flames were licking in from the gardens,

Visionary flowers, you were witnesses to the Last Judgment

Visionary flowers, you last for the space of a word.

Why this great fire, Miguel?

No, no, I wasn't thinking about that, Montserrat said.

I said to her then: "Tell me what you have chosen."

You know, my love, you know that it is you.

Then do not leave me.

If I am to come back to you, then I must leave you first

I shall be carried away like a wave; see, I am already sliding from you

In the glowing heat of the stones,

The pillars are collapsing and I can see myself enmeshed in their lines of fire,

The flames or me,

See,

You, Miguel, you

Where will the smoking chapels go

Where will the windows go to hide their gaping wounds?

Where will Montserrat go—ravaged now?

　　　　　　　　With you

To the East

A cathedral knelt down in the ashes.

For days and for nights we were kept apart.

"You, you, Miguel, I have already told you."

Montserrat was looking at him. Both turned to stone on the threshold of Bourges cathedral, they were speaking to each other gently, face to face. And the woman saw that the man was weeping.

I stretched myself out beside her on the brazen tomb, and we waited for night to fall.

TUESDAY NIGHT

Dear Johann,

I beg of you to withdraw from Montserrat's life and from mine. You do not realize the danger that you represent for us: the chance of paradise you seem is as falsely enchanting as all illusions are. Yes, you must free us of that danger. We have tried to escape from it in France's cathedrals; we have attempted to free our spirits from their bondage. (For have you not bewitched us?) We set out on a crusade to free our souls, and do you know what we have discovered? You, Johann, everywhere and in everything: your presence . . .

What a deception!

Tomorrow, Wednesday, I am asking you to leave at

dawn. My wife and I need a few more days of peace still before our triumph in Venice next Sunday. Before you came into our life, we were each other's lovers enough to be lovers of life as well.

We never thought of death. She loved me. I loved her, and because of our simple happiness in the perfect understanding between us, I was enough for her and she was enough for me. We had no other thirst, no other hunger. We were making our journey toward the end of our days. Our descent from the heights was unsullied. We were sated and freed from ecstasy. Then, suddenly, Montserrat saw in you a sublime temptation whose meaning I do not understand—and the same was true for me, though on another plane, I believe. She knew thirst again. And I knew hunger. We were separated from one another. We were afraid, in Chartres, in Bourges, on tombs of bronze, or brass, or stone; we longed to find our way back to the bodies we had lost; we moaned over our scattered limbs . . . In short, you have inspired us with such greatness of soul, a greatness of soul so wild and untamable, that it has made us crush out all our desires.

You may perhaps be one of the race of Immortals (like those magnificent angels I have seen at Chartres, standing beside Montserrat, with her head resting on my shoulder) and this temptation is also a temptation to seek immortality, a temptation that comes from you, from your words, from your voice, which is too pure, too searing in our ears—but we shall not give way to it, we prefer to live and to die, or to go on dying forever and never be reborn. We decided that when we were still children, she and I, in Madrid, one day of summer heat when I uncovered the rose of her shoulder for the first time . . .

All this I understood last Sunday, as the curtain fell after the final scene of my play. There was a wonderful, a dismal twilight then: the twilight of the void. She fears all resurrections of the past. She is afraid to see me appear through her. That is Montserrat. When I wonder sometimes why Montserrat's eyes become so beautiful toward the end of the day, I discover at once that those eyes of hers are the two tranquil ghosts of everything that is not and of everything that never was, of everything that has known the piercing pain of not knowing how to exist. Montserrat is mortal. Like myself.

We are strangers, you and I, even supposing that our two lives obey the same law of creation. And everything that you create bears the stamp of your immortality, whereas for Montserrat and me, on the contrary, every work we accomplish decomposes always beneath our fingers as fast as we can make it. I know what you think.

You saw Montserrat take a sketch, apply her magic, and throw off a splendid, virile forehead, or the triumph in a young woman's eyes, or the shadowed curve of a child's mouth. But those sculptures were merely transients on this earth: today, this instant, even as I write this to you, they are already destroying themselves on their own, like everything produced by mortal man. We are decaying at every moment of our lives, together with all that we are. We have no idols apart from this religious love with which we worship one another, and it is a cult shorn of frenzy. It is calmer and wiser than the desert. I am not complaining that we are what we are. But I am begging you to leave us what is ours, what has always been ours, through the ages. Though we have no future life, still we have had the lives we have already lived, and they are the secrets and the bonds of our existence today.

Montserrat doesn't know what she is doing: she sees you as a diabolical presence . . . The being who can tempt another thus far can only be an angel, and I have always trembled more at the thought of angels than at the thought of the devil. I am afraid of an angel's persecution.

Think back to our first meeting, and to Montserrat as she lay coiled and smiling in the half darkness of our apartment. Montserrat languishing as she listened to you.

"Miguel, recite that poem for us, darling . . ."

Listen to her supple voice and the sudden, unexpected progress of her body along the wall. She had left the shadow so as to see you better. She was seeing the devil. I knew from the unknowing reflections in her eyes.

"Miguel! Come on!"

> Of this body stretched out by my side
> I long to see the soul a single time
> To seize it at last like a wounded sun
> Hold it in an irrecoverable embrace
> Deep in its void . . .

Listen to Montserrat as she goes on, inert once more before you, listen . . .

> Autumn breath on my lonely brow
> You do not know who my love is,
> You do not know where I live
> Your long snowy eyes
> Offer me no directions
> You do not know for whom I weep
> Or of whom I sing
> If you did not exist already, O incoherent earth
> I would go and look for you in God

Autumn breath on my lonely brow
I am hurling myself at last into the original fire!
I wandered hopeless once, from one wind to the next
Battered by the heavens' hurricane
I wandered hopeless once from one wind to the next
Weep now, weep, O living being!
I have veiled the too naked soul
Of this body stretched out by my side . . .

"Be quiet," I said to Montserrat. Yet, though she ceased to speak, she went on waiting for something with rebellion in her heart. At last she spoke again. (I had moved away from you both to give more attention to the rain falling on Paris; my whole being was sad and frozen, I wanted to hear you laughing together, to ravel out the angel laughter from the confused, confusing woman's laughter. But I could make out nothing. Those few words from Montserrat, perhaps . . .)

"Yes, I am moved too when I think of his writing. But, Johann . . ." (No, she repeated your name with despair in her voice) "Johann, my friend, he doesn't know what he is saying. He doesn't know that all those words add up to so little. He doesn't know how or why those lines are inspired in him, or by whom, and I don't want him to find out: all he ever writes is his condition as a mortal man, he writes with ashes and we live with our blood" (She had one hand on her breast and must have felt her heart beating within her, like a young girl when she is thinking) "Johann! Johann! What pain he is going to feel tomorrow!" (The beating of her heart became suddenly irregular, and for a moment she looked like the old woman she would never have the time to become) "Let us drive all pain away, Johann! My husband writes so many words without knowing their true weight. Even when he was still only a little boy, he used to write out the deaths of bulls in his school exercise books, and that was the first time I saw blood flow, leaning over him as his black pen drew the outlines of those huge, red words. And then I forgot. I was with him at the university in Rome, though I don't remember its name (ask him; he knows everything about our past, but I forget)— while he wrote words even more terrible still, during the great anonymous vengeance of the war. But he also knew how to write down the song of fountains, the laments of men when half asleep, so many dead or dying things!"

"Yes, that untamed adolescent, I saw him going by at one time, in the streets of Rome . . ."

The wind was rippling over Montserrat's hair. (At that point, I came and closed all the doors.) I felt myself leaning over Montserrat's warm neck. But it was only in my thoughts.

"Miguel, how cool it is suddenly!"

You were there, you were still there, spying on me without knowing it.

WEDNESDAY — RHEIMS CATHEDRAL

Miguel, Miguel, recite that poem to me, so that I shall remember you until I die, perhaps it will be possible, Miguel, Miguel, if you will it so for me to remember you even beyond death, and then you yourself would be my immortality, for there is no other I would wish for myself.

Yes, my desire is that your body shall forget nothing, never forget, forget nothing of what is now my soul

Miguel Miguel, like my mother as she lay dying alone and without God. And they asked her, Whom do you wish to see? Whom do you wish to love? This is the final moment and eternity is here

Soon everything will be finished, so open your eyes now to what will never end, and do you know what the dying woman replied?

May my body forget nothing, never forget, forget nothing of what is now my soul

"My mother was young, very young still, the day she died," Montserrat said. "No one knew that as well as I."

Where is my lover? Where is my husband?

Whereupon my father went to her and took her hand.

"Montserrat," he said, "it is no longer permissible for me to go on living in the sight of God."

"Be silent," Miguel said.

He placed his hand over Montserrat's mouth and held it closed.

"Be silent," he begged, with startled gentleness.

He took away his hand. Montserrat looked at him. His eyes were keeping watch through the silence of the night.

"Sometimes, Miguel, you confuse what I tell you within you and what I am thinking, far away from you."

"Yes," Miguel said humbly.

"Sometimes, Miguel, you confuse what you write with what you see."

"Yes," Miguel said.

"Please, Miguel, confess that poem to me for the very last time. And tell me what you saw in the cathedral at Rheims."

"I think I prayed there," Miguel said.

Montserrat pressed her lips together in the effort to ward off any interruption to her thought.

In the cathedral at Rheims

> That morning in May
> They were crowning a king . . .
> See the tall Angel bending low . . .
> See the tall Angel stooping there . . .

"It is the year 1328. We are about to see the coronation of Philippe VI . . ."

"The king I am telling of knows nothing of his power."

The king I am telling of is only a child. Time does not exist for him.

> See the tall Angel bending low . . .
> In the cathedral at Rheims
> That morning in May
> They sacrificed a child

No, Miguel, no! You know very well that all that was happening only in your mind. We had scarcely walked in through the great doorway when we saw a host of children coming toward us. Children at their first communion in the month of May, like an expanse of lilies opening into bloom on some fabled horizon.

I said to him, "Miguel, stay with me." But he let himself be carried away in that majestic unfolding of pure white wings. He was foundering at the center of my soul.

Miguel. Miguel.

In the cathedral of Rheims, which I gazed at like some past and buried age—I saw the terror of unity and the singing city of symmetry pass before me,

Surrounded by so many vast proportions, I saw the passions of men blow past me like winds of light,

Harmony itself had been set upon the features of the great Angel overhead,

> O cruel Wind, O tender Wind
> The winds of the Last Judgment were blowing by.

No, Montserrat, no, my darling! You know very well that all those things existed only in your mind.

"Perhaps you are right, Miguel."

I said to him, "Miguel, do not leave me."

The cathedral stood above the town
The cathedral stood above the world,
Miguel, I am only the lover of all that,
It would be better if you didn't leave me,
Gallery of prophets,
One would say that God is thinking. Look, Miguel.
No, Montserrat, no, that is the transparent frenzy of
   your mind.
A row of white flagstones with borders of black stone
And the children walking and their shadows flying
Is that a dream, Miguel?
All of it was simply a dream in your mind, Montserrat.
Montserrat's mind is a vale where every gay disorder
   blooms.
And yet I saw them clearly enough, Montserrat, those
   labyrinths
And those high vaults streaming with the transparency
   of heaven
Miguel. Miguel. You were in exile. You saw nothing.
And the six towers. And the seven black staircases of
   marble
And the columns as slender as dawns
And that rose, Miguel, that rose with its six lobes
Opening toward the West.

It has closed again since. All of it was beauty in your mind, only that.

"Tell me the poem," Montserrat begged.

"Yes," Miguel said.

The man's voice was burning his blood, lonely waterfall of laments.

Andantino. His blood being burned by the woman's memory.

> In Rheims cathedral
> On this May morning
> The melancholy child is silent
> As they come to place the thorns upon his head
> In Rheims cathedral
> "Say nothing to his mother
> As she weaves in a distant house.
> Say nothing to his mother."
> On the infant's forehead now there flows
> The first red snow of his own young blood
> But say nothing to his mother
> As she weaves for her son
> In a far-away house
> Though the boy is going to die today
> In Rheims cathedral
> He is the prince of sacrifice
> There is no day but some child dies
> In a cathedral
> There is no day but to let you live
> A carnation dies in the dew, Montserrat.
> There is no hour but to let you live
> A child is swallowed by the ocean's spray, Miguel.
> I am weaving the tunic of pearls
> That he will wear next day.
> Say nothing to his mother
> As she hems his delicate robe of death,
> So that you may love, Montserrat.
> The warm dew of the infant's blood

Is falling now onto his fingers
And generous, heartbroken hands
Lay on the necklaces of thorns
O Briars, you weep
When the thoughtful child
Dares not murmur
As his eyelids droop
As the first bloody drops of mourning dew
Fall on his childish hands.
I am weaving the silken robe
That my son will soil in the morning.
Say nothing to his mother. Don't let her know.
What has become of the nightingale
In our house?
Could it not come and find me here
The winged moon messenger
Could it not come and share my pain
Where has it gone, into what oblivion,
The nightingale?
I am dying for a being who does not know me yet
No hour passes but a child
Finds itself the captive of an unresolved redemption
What has become of the nightingale
In our house?
Why can't it come and find me here?
Crucify him
Who was it who said that?
You or I, Montserrat
You or I, Miguel
On this May morning
The child has been stripped of all its vestments
(And at that moment his mother, bent over the tunic she

was sewing, saw a drop of blood oozing out, like a tear fallen onto the hollow of a living mirror)

Trembling on the threshold of grace
And nakedness
The child is abandoned to the South
Riven with pain
Say nothing to his mother
Who thinks he is asleep in the nightingale wood
Say nothing to his mother
Who thinks he is being dazzled
By a mirage of fountains in Jerusalem
(Already, already, she is forgetting the drop of blood)
They are crucifying the child
In Rheims cathedral,
They are driving nails through his feet and his hands
They are crucifying the child
In the cathedral of France
And on his bleeding side
The first snows of death are spreading
At last.
(Already, already, she is forgetting her child's death)
Montserrat opened her eyes. The man's voice fell silent.

"Darling," she said, "this Poem of the Passion never existed anywhere but in your mind."

"Perhaps," Miguel said.

"It was only a dream."

"I'm afraid," Montserrat said. "Because it could be true too."

She was remembering how their day in Rheims ended. She had found Miguel again. She had knelt in front of him, and she had said: "I am afraid of loving you too much." He had stroked the back of her neck as it bowed to his rhythmic touch. "Miguel, you're listening to what I say, aren't you? I'm afraid of taking up all the room inside you. How can I explain, I mean the forbidden room, the part that is God's."

"That doesn't matter," Miguel had said.

And in the train, as they were traveling back toward Paris, he said the same words again, wholly without anguish.

"Don't you realize what it is I'm saying to you, Miguel?"

"Montserrat, there's nothing to be afraid of. I know what I want."

Abruptly, several young people burst into the compartment. Miguel turned away his face, like a man who has grown weary of himself. Montserrat recognized the pianist and her fiancé, Jean, together with the children who had sung all day in the cathedral.

"You do remember us, don't you? This is Miguel. I am Montserrat. Were you in Rheims today?"

"Yes," the girl said, "my fiancé set a poem to music, in the cathedral."

Then she turned to Miguel and inquired: "Where have you been?"

"If only I knew," Miguel said.

Moment Two

"Thursday, your face belongs to me and I do not know it all."

Allegro Ma Non Troppo.

On that Sunday in May, in Paris, at the beginning of the third movement, Montserrat felt her heart grow weak— her gaze was troubled as she enjoyed a kind of vaporous dizziness. She had always been the friend of everything alive and therefore of the heart that was now damming up the tumult of her blood. She had betrothed herself to its unfailing regularity just as she had betrothed herself to Miguel's heart and to the tireless dimension of his being.

"My heart is too slow. You are so slow."

"What did you say?" Miguel asked. "What is it?"

On Miguel's deserted profile, she could see her own absorbed, reflective face: in the same way, Miguel had lifted his hand to his heart with the thought: "My blood is draining out of me. I shall be dying soon."

"Be quiet darling," Miguel said.

Suddenly Montserrat recalled at what moment, on what day, she had already felt the power of this mute distress, this deep abandon of the body as it withdraws itself from the soul (before the soul can withdraw itself from the body). Yes, on Thursday, at eight o'clock, in Johann's arms.

Allegro Ma Non Troppo.

The end of this movement would be the end of Montserrat. She knew it. Johann was playing on inside his blessed garment of simplicity. All that he knew, and all he did not know, of this meditative movement was melting together within him, under the humble power of his hands; he was the eagle and the eagle's prey, finding himself, yet losing himself at every instant.

Allegro Ma Non Troppo.

Such were Montserrat's thoughts as she sat beside her husband.

Miguel, still trembling within at the week she had just lived through, transfixed forever by a revelation out of all proportion to her own self.

"Yes, Thursday, that face."

THURSDAY

"What have you done with Miguel?"

"He's out walking by the river."

"In this rain?"

"In this rain, yes."

He took Montserrat's hands, then opened them on the bedside table, in the vertical glow of the lamp.

"I can see an infinity of wounds, here in your hands. Why?"

"I have been making a cape for Miguel all day. Those are the marks of the needles you see on my hand."

She laughed.

"Why torture your hands?"

"Poor Johann, what are my hands good for, except making capes for Miguel?"

"And these sculptures?"

He gestured toward the tall, static figures that were surrounding them, pressing in on them from every side, like the ghosts of their shadowed love.

"I didn't really make those," Montserrat said.

"Then where did they come from?"

"You know the answer to that better than I do," Montserrat said, "so don't interrogate me any more."

There came three days to parallel the first three days. Monday and Tuesday, then Wednesday, had been given over to pursuits and storms in the cathedrals of France— now they were entering upon the three days of shipwreck. The pendulum of time was indifferent to this abrupt precipitation. Montserrat had been through three days of despair, so there was no reason why she should not now cull, in their turn—from out of the vast blanketing fall of days that had still to cover the unquiet earth—these three further and too brief days, the days that were to flood her flesh with hope before watching her dissolve into the void. At last, Johann had come to share that diabolical hope, and there was nothing more she asked. Yes, one other thing perhaps: not to forget Miguel, to remain at his service until death. And to love him more than herself even when he had become no more than the small pile of ashes she was imagining already at the end of his life, that fistful of rustling ashes in her palm . . .

"At first a woman starts to wither in her hands, then in her lips . . ."

"I don't know how one dies," Montserrat said, cruelly.

"Where are you, Montserrat? Where are you, so un-faithful and yet so faithful, Montserrat?"

"I know where we are, Johann. At the heart of the flood, in Paris. The other houses are succumbing and being swal-lowed by the waters. Our house is standing firm. Yes, I know all that. I have known it for a long time now. But I am lying, Johann. What interests me in all this is you. Your secret. And you won't speak it; even in your sleep you will keep silence. This body that you are . . . Ah! You think that is all I need! No, I am too much aware of all it hides from me. As a child, I was hungry. They gave me bread. And that bread was not magical enough to sate my hunger. It is the same now with you. You are an angel or a demon; but if you are not the one or the other, then you do not exist."

"I am a man," Johann said. "You must give up this stubborn insistence on believing otherwise."

(And more gently, folding Montserrat's hands closed again and holding them between his own, as one covers over the agile surface of a thing too vulnerable to contacts)

"Montserrat, I too would like to know who you are!"

"But what can it be you want to know, Johann? Yes, I have lived only for him. But what of it? Is there a penalty more than death for having loved so much? Take care of him. Don't tempt him with that strange immortality. I can feel it inside him, that temptation. The desire to escape from me in order to penetrate deeper into time. (Isn't love the God of lost time?) That's all I can be for him, nothing else. What have you done to him? Why did you come?

Why did I pursue you? As a child, I can remember having longed to know you . . . to see your eyes, to have you take me. Yes, I willed it. But why? Was it absurd? And you are lit with the glory of all that we shall never be. Your happy calm is our stern judge."

"Montserrat, I think I see that you are in fear of your body's ending. For you believe that there will be no new beginning afterwards."

"No, none. But take me again now, so I can draw from you for an instant—one instant only, if that is within your power (the devil's beauty is all-powerful)—that inward eternity soon to be ravished from me."

"No," Johann said. "Go away from me."

Montserrat entered into the embrace as into a tomb, closed her eyes, saw her long and lightning-stricken limbs stretched out outside herself, savored the releasing fall—uncoiling into vastness—and little by little became the heaving plain, motionless an instant and instantly rising up again, destroyed and delivered still by the winds of pleasure, and struck once again into an amazement as still as modesty. Then came the vague happiness of sleep, catching her by surprise: one by one, the half-open roses of her fingers closed; imperceptibly, the blond flesh, like a bird in the heavy grip of vertigo, sank in upon itself and refused any further, shuddering caress. So does the gilded maize shrink from the burning sun.

Her neck and head sank unprotesting back into the delicious void, like a tree as it slides majestically down into a wide green silence that is nothing like the silence of distress. The shoulders and the breasts of Montserrat were the tragic bark of that tall tree (they could be seen separating themselves from the tree, stretching out, hiding themselves, abrupt and ever-changing), while her blood continued to feed it like a secret sap, the sacred river at the origin of things. And her legs were already rising upwards like some sumptuous sacrifice on a bed of black and burning coals.

Montserrat was asleep in that embrace, at the heart of a tomb at the heart of a tree, and she would not dare to sully with even a single cry the mourning formed around her by the thin forest of the world.

As she awoke, she felt the wounds of love growing within her. The Moment was already another past. Johann was a simulacrum of silence, stretched out on his side, his body seemingly posed as though across the absent body from which he had separated himself such a short while before, with the real cruelty of memory.

"Johann," Montserrat murmured. "Johann."

But he couldn't have heard her. She found herself alone, and her heart began to beat very slowly. How was she to summon it back to life, to restore its warmth?

"You're leaving me, you're leaving me, you're all I have, oh living heart."

As she sat beside the man, Montserrat knew that she had just been drawn from his side, and she did not take that sleep away, because she knew that she had always been a wound in that sleep.

"Johann, Johann, you rule over my bones,
I rule over your blood,
We are but one single being
In the region beyond our will,
Which does not last . . ."

As she leaned there on her pale flank, the woman was discovering, perhaps, as though she looked down into a diaphanous stream, the secret of a fragile misery which had come into being at the same moment as herself. She asked no more than to efface herself before the mystery of an estrangement too sweet to bear: estrangement from man's misfortune.

"Now," Montserrat thought, "now I shall be able to take Miguel in my arms and instill in him this strength, this luminous power that I can sense in the depths of myself, or rather these absolute forms of darkness that are dazzling me."

"Johann, listen to me!"

He opened his eyes and complained to find his body shackled so. "Montserrat, who has been here and robbed me of part of my flesh?"

"I have," Montserrat answered. "While you slept."

"You knew that it would cause me pain," Johann said.

"Yes, I knew," Montserrat said.

Toward the end of the evening, Montserrat was sculpting Johann's face. The approaching coolness of the night revived her weary fingers, and Montserrat was able to create a man.

"What's the matter, Montserrat?"

"Nothing, Johann, nothing. But this is my last work and I shall leave my own life in it. Why should that worry you? As you draw life from me, so I die. I have to leave you the light in my eyes . . . I have to make sure . . ."

"Oh, be silent," Johann begged. "You're so tired, my love."

No tear would spring from Montserrat's now burned-out eyes.

"Yes, I am very tired," she said.

THURSDAY NIGHT

"Miguel! Miguel!"

Montserrat had waited for him on the thresholds of all the houses in Paris. She had run along the quais. She had kept watch for him at the night-filled métro exit. Miguel was no longer there. He was continuing his terror-stricken hunt, the chase that had led him as far afield as Bourges. He was searching for a way to pull the vast lament of Paris down on top of him.

"Miguel!"

Suddenly she saw him, panting and alone. She took his arm and begged him to go back with her to the house. The rain was turning to ice along the streets.

"And you're chilled through, Miguel. We'll light a nice fire in our room. . ."

She was smiling at him as she used to do before, as she had on Monday, on the way back from Chartres.

"If you knew how hungry I am for the feel of you in my arms," Miguel said.

"Have you been searching for the angel, Miguel?"

"No, I have been fleeing from him," he said.

"And tomorrow, Miguel?"

"I shall flee him still," he said. "And you?"

"I have found what I was seeking. I should like to draw so close to it that I need never move away from it again."

"And tomorrow, Montserrat?"

"I shall go back to it again—" said Montserrat.

They stood facing the five flights of iron stairs separating them from their apartment, from the locked doors of their rooms.

"We shall never get that far," Montserrat said.

Then, in triumph, Miguel took her in his arms and climbed each step with a fragile quarry that did not lift its gaze from him, buried in the hollow of his shoulder, grateful and faithful to this secret wedding night.

Leaning down toward the fire that was warming the whole room, Montserrat sat rubbing her hands together, alert to Miguel's presence by her side.

"What have you done to your hands and your eyes, Montserrat?"

"Yes, you will ask me that every day, Miguel. I am going to grow old now very ardently. You must pay no attention to me. Am I so ugly, now that I've begun to die?"

"No," Miguel said.

"With those great hands—now raise me up, yes, I am about to perish."

Miguel had taken pity on the words that Montserrat had spoken.

And from this other embrace he rose up again with pain in his heart.

THE DREAM OF SPAIN

"You were ten, Montserrat, or eight perhaps
I saw you for the first time in a church in Barcelona
Keep her away from me, I said to my mother and my
    sisters
She is too beautiful to make me desire her
She is too gentle to love me
But I already knew that Montserrat
Across the whole world would wait for me
With that same fatal smile"

"Tell me, why is the Virgin busy spinning
When the Angel messenger comes?
Tell me why . . ."
I said nothing then, Montserrat.
You were nine, Montserrat, or perhaps thirteen
When you came up to me during that pilgrimage to
    the Virgin
It was on a starbright night in Montserrat
I put my arm tight around your waist then
We were alone among the silent crowds
"Pray with me, pray with me in Montserrat."
                    I didn't pray
I saw Miguel in Barcelona in a garden
In the middle of the sea
We slept in a boat in the evenings
And as each dawn broke we found ourselves together
In the bay of Palma de Mallorca,
The silvered hills were fading
And then appeared the port, while rising in the
    distance,
Like a mountain,
                    Was the cathedral . . .
"Which was the church in Barcelona?"
"Santa María del Pina."
"No," Miguel said, "it was at Santa María del Mar. In
    May."
"Tell me, why is the Virgin busy spinning
When the Angel messenger comes?
Tell me why." But he didn't tell me.
My mother's face was veiled in black.
"Keep away, Miguel, walk with your sisters, Miguel."
We were going to Avila

My mother's hands were veiled in blue
My sisters had on skirts as deep as the sky
And you could see stars and flowers in them
Traced with a needle
I loved the hollow curves of their nimble waists
We were going to Avila
Along the way, there were old women
Laying their weary heads against the setting sun
And breathing calmly
"Miguel, Miguel, why are you crying, Miguel?"
Dark and faithful light
Our little donkey blinked his eyes
At every well, at every step.
You were ten, Montserrat, or perhaps seven
When I saw you walk toward me, straight-backed,
     magnificent,
You came to your innocent executioner eyes closed
Not knowing that he would bind you forever to that
     setting sun
Of Avila
As well as to the bleeding passion of his heart.
"There the mountains rose around us like thickets of
     thorns,
And sad gray olive trees were bent to the winds."
"No," Miguel said, "there were only the olive trees
     rising
Into the austere solitude
As unlooked for as the lament of a harp . . ."
"Tell me, why is the Virgin busy spinning
When the Angel messenger comes?"
In that distant, that very distant church in Barcelona
I said nothing, Montserrat.

Take me to Madrid
Go away from me
Aren't we betrothed?
Take me to Madrid
You're not fifteen yet
Madrid, the church of San Josué.
"Tell me, why is the Virgin busy spinning
When the Angel messenger comes?"
In the Plaza Monumental
A corrida or a flight of stars?
Miguel thought of nothing but me and I thought of
    nothing but him
From him to me the only distance
Was the flutter of a fan.
"Fold up that fan, you're hiding your eyes from me"
But I wasn't listening to him, so as to think of him
    better
"Cruel girl, what are you about? Ah, what a woman
    you are!"
I wanted to have him understand that other distance
That would always exist as well
"Did you understand, Miguel?"
"No, later, much later."
"You're making me feverish, Montserrat. Listen to
    me."
We appeared as one in the eyes of men
And God likewise had made us inseparable
"An infinite distance, O Montserrat."
And that distance alone was enough to tear the world
    apart
"Lower your fan, you are making me thirsty for the
    sight of you."

Fire and shadow—she raised and lowered the fan
And I never once knew the quiet of her eyes.
A corrida or a flight of stars?
The alguazils rode by in procession on their horses, the
    picadors
And the banderilleros
All made ready for the banquet of agony
And I had nothing but Montserrat
Who was making me die a thousand deaths,
Uninterrupted mistress of my life . . .
The picadors on their horses were the first
To bury their thrusts in the almost willing victim
He grows weaker, I am in pain, my blood streams out,
    I am in pain
No, Montserrat. No
The banderilleros are renewing his torture
They move up to him and inflict their glancing, insidi-
    ous torment
"With the oppressed, you also bow your head.
With the strong you stand tall again."
Yes, said Miguel.
No, listen to me, Montserrat, your eyes
Already it was time for the pass of death
And the matador was expecting his triumph
The fan fell then from her burning fingers
Miguel, why do you weep?
"I have understood that infinite distance at last,"
    Miguel said.

The Final Moment

FRIDAY — THE DREAM OF PARIS

From the Ile Saint-Louis they could see the apse of Notre Dame, a perfect whole of glittering stones. Cruel and swift as the departing flight of a swan at night, Montserrat's voice sailed toward Miguel's cheek and then was gone.

"No, you haven't understood that infinite distance, Miguel. You know nothing about it, even now."

"Did you hear me talking to you in my dream then, Montserrat?"

"Yes."

"Don't be sad, Montserrat. It was only the dream of a dream."

"I heard it all," Montserrat said.

"Be good, Montserrat."

"Remember, Miguel, in Granada, how everything separated us from one another. The color of the sky, the color of the water, the word a child spoke inside a house, the gaze of a woman we did not know—forgive me, I still feel that great separation from you even now. I don't know where the feeling comes from."

From time to time the rain on Miguel's brow drifted like a balm of snow.

"I feel no pain," Miguel said. "I feel nothing at all any more."

And I don't understand what that means: "to be separated from someone you love." Why should you be separated from me? We are together.

"I know that you were humiliated, Miguel, on Sunday, the day your play opened."

"I have forgotten now," Miguel said.

"You were humiliated too by the knowledge that Johann would never understand you."

"Perhaps," Miguel said, "but really I have forgotten everything else, so that I can think of you alone."

> When there were horse races on Sunday
> I came and sat down by him in the gardens
> We were alone beneath the vast spread of the moon-
>   light
> Gazing at those mysterious cavalcades
> The pale and noble horses hurtling past on their
>   straight course
> To drown themselves in the gold of the cornfields
> Miguel, Miguel
> White horses
> Running on the frozen river

"What are you doing," Miguel asked. "Yes, why are you hiding your face with your umbrella? You know very well how much I need to see you."

> When there were horse races on Sunday
> I came and sat down by him in the gardens in Sara-
>   gossa.
> And our parents would say of us:
> "Let us leave those tragic children there in peace,
> For they belong each one to the other

All through the ages."
Fire and shadow—I never once knew the quiet of your
eyes.
Racing horses or racing stars
I climbed up on his horse, with how delicate a hand
He seized hold of me so as to feel I was his,
And yet when he opened his fingers
That was enough to lose me.
Montserrat, Montserrat, he said. I moved my lips near
to his mouth
Miguel, Miguel, I said to him
You are the fisherman of the rising sun
And he laughed
Racing horses or racing stars
I no longer came to sit down by him
On Sunday in Saragossa, for we had grown up
And we were beings of the universe.
And the autumn wind like his laugh
Was sailing from branch to branch
"I want to see you," Miguel begged.
The umbrella fell from Montserrat's burning fingers
"It's nothing Miguel, nothing at all. I'm here."
And she heard him laugh—as he had in their youth.

FRIDAY NIGHT

Montserrat, her arms cast adrift on both sides of her, like
the hull of a boat pushing aside the high-rearing pressures
of wave and spume, was sliding down, from silence into
silence, toward the abyss of an astonished mindlessness,
only opening her eyes from time to time to remind herself—with caution—that Miguel still existed.

"Why spend so long sewing, Montserrat? You carry so many years now within you, Montserrat."

"And you, Miguel, what is it you're trying to do? You know well enough that temptations cannot be killed."

Miguel drew aside the curtains and looked at the creations of the darkness, those barren statues born of Montserrat's nimble spirit, spreading, unfolding their gilded and secret warmth till it reached Miguel's tranquil eyes. Finally, that warmth penetrated Miguel's body and soul as well, and he recognized the dark grip of a thought binding him to every object created by her hands. And he was disturbed.

"What is it you're trying to do, Miguel?"

Montserrat's supplication reached his ears like a timorous lament, penetrated him, and stirred up the violence within him.

"Why kill your brother Cain? Can you not hear God's anguish?"

But those statues that had been the beloved sisters of his life and Montserrat's own children (a perfect obedience in the gaze of each and every figure) had suddenly ceased to express that supreme submission to Miguel's will: suddenly they were turning against him. Miguel could see them, inimical, incomprehensible, pressing in on him from every side. One of them was destroying all of them. One of them, Johann . . .

"What are you doing, Miguel? What is it you're trying to do?"

O Miguel, what a dismal victory you have won! Kneeling among the fragments of that shattered figure! Miguel, Miguel!

Night had fallen. Montserrat could hear the rain drumming on the roofs of Paris. The sound awakened such an echo deep inside her that she felt herself come to life. She raised herself up, bringing her arms down to her sides.

"How well I feel," she cried.

"Forgive me, my darling," Miguel said. "I will mend it all."

"No, Miguel, there is no point. I like the pieces better. Look . . . the petals of a rose."

"A flower," Miguel said.

"The end of our springtime," Montserrat said.

She was discovering the unfathomable sadness of discovering herself to be exactly like him, already consumed in the ashes soon to come.

THE SATURDAY

Allegro Ma Non Troppo

"It's tomorrow, isn't it, Johann? Sunday? Why haven't you gone already?"

"Tomorrow is the day I play," Johann said. "You know how serious all this is for me. I have been preparing myself to play this concerto well for months."

"For years," the woman sighed, shrugging her shoulders. Montserrat huddled back against the wall as she listened to Johann speak. She was drawing back up into her memory all the debris of their strange adventure; searching in darkness for the necessity of this sensual escstasy that had hurled her—like some object utterly pure and utterly sullied at the same time—into Johann's hands.

"Do what you will with me . . ."

"That is a monstrous thing to say. It would be better to unsay it."

"I cannot keep it unsaid," Montserrat cried rebelliously.

Already he was no longer the man she had held back from the brink of eternity; Johann's soul had come to the rescue of Johann's body. That radiant and feeling soul . . .

"No, I will not unsay it," she said.

Allegro Ma Non Troppo

Johann was still playing. What she saw burning in his eyes no longer had a name. The inner vibration of his being no longer possessed that wild or tranquil reverberation that had astonished Montserrat's memory only yesterday. Everything was crumbling away.

Johann had been blasted and felled by Miguel's right arm.

"Will you think of me in Vienna?"

"Yes," he said.

"And tomorrow, in Venice, in the eternal city?"

"Yes, Montserrat."

"How you lie! You have already forgotten that embrace, the embrace that makes a woman suddenly aware that she is destined for a man, destined for his body, for his desire; you have forgotten that embrace as we stood in Paris in the rain and the darkness of this month of May and how the form of your whole body seized me and surprised me amazed me attracted me ravished me at last still standing without a movement with your hand resting on my neck and I could see you better and more gently you have forgotten Johann and I went quickly away to be with Miguel in my room and I embraced him in the same way and I understood everything anew Miguel smiled he rested his hand on my neck and I closed my eyes.

Allegro Ma Non Troppo

"Come closer, Montserrat."

She obeyed. He laid his hand on Montserrat's breast and closed his eyes.

"That heart, that poor heart . . ."

In the Place de l'Opéra, Miguel watched the vast and riven azure rise around him. He had stood shaken in the same way once before—shaken and ravished by the Mediterranean's miraculous expanse.

Montserrat. Montserrat.

He would wait for her here. She would come to him perhaps, or else she would never come again. And the first time he had seen Montserrat he had been filled with desire for the Mediterranean, for the sea, for her eyes, for Montserrat's Mediterranean eyes. And everything had grown calm inside him at that moment. Montserrat had conquered him with a single gesture of one finger, with a single movement of her shoulder. How he regretted having loved so much! How tired he felt!

You won't be cold in this cape my love

You won't feel any more pain

You can travel on to the end of the earth.

How many days did it take you to make this cape, Montserrat?

One day was enough

He was walking toward the invisible figure of Montserrat (that fiery figure that once, in time past, sent all the suns of Spain into eclipse), Montserrat preparing to come to him, to rush in on him from every side, Montserrat and her comradely step.

"Nearer, Montserrat, nearer, I beg of you . . ."

Miguel was glad to feel himself a slave to the last day of the world.

The rain was still streaming over his empty limbs.

Soon he became aware that his heart was an open chalice.

The blood was running down over his clothes.

You won't feel the pain any more in this cape, my love . . .

"Weren't you waiting for me then, Miguel?"

She was there, without sadness and without strength.

"Miguel, your heart, your poor heart . . ."

She laid her hand on Miguel's breast and closed her eyes.

Allegro Ma Non Troppo

Such was the end of the last movement. Johann stood up. His hour of triumph exploded like an unspeakable roar in that Paris concert hall, on that Sunday, the third day of May.

Montserrat tried to turn back toward Miguel, but he was no longer at her side.

Some while later, Montserrat went up to Johann. He seized her by the hands. "No, Montserrat, wishing to say goodbye to everything is wrong."

"But that is what I wish," she said.

"And Miguel?"

"I shall find him again."

He watched her go. He was thinking of her, and of a great many other things at the same time. He was happy. He had just been told of the birth of his second child. There was his hope of going back to Vienna soon, there was his hope . . .

And the Seine had already ferried away the soul and the body of Miguel. He was lying alone in the troubled waters. Running along the quais, Montserrat was hastening toward the same great flow . . . To open Miguel's tomb and rest beside him.

The deluge over Paris ceased.

The Place de l'Opéra burst into flames in a moment. Montserrat could not but perish there, without the knowledge of the man she had loved.

And in Vienna it was snowing that day, and Johann's child was coming into the world.

Other Titles In This Series

Sara Jeannette Duncan

THE POOL IN THE DESERT

Sara Jeannette Duncan was the first Canadian woman to achieve international success as a journalist, novelist, and travel writer. Born in 1861, she wrote more than twenty books during a career which took her to the Far East, India, and England.

First published in 1903, the four novellas in this collection are told with a fine sense of irony and sophistication. Set against the backdrop of British India these vividly rendered portraits of women who attempt to defy convention are as fresh and provocative today as when they were written.

"These stories are told with much cleverness and subtlety in the elusive, fine-drawn style of Henry James."

The New York Times 1903

". . . one of Canada's most rewarding writers. She is astute in conception, deft in execution and thoroughly entertaining."

Books in Canada

Timothy Findley

DINNER ALONG THE AMAZON

The sound of screen doors banging, evening lamplight: Colt revolvers hidden in bureau drawers and a chair that is always falling over.

These are the sounds and images that illuminate this brilliant collection of twelve short stories from one of Canada's finest writers.

The stories range from the powerful, haunting *Lemonade*, where a young boy's world is shattered by his mother's self destruction, to the title story, an unusual journey into the complexities of modern relationships, written especially for this collection.

"Timothy Findley is one of Canada's most original and important writers...He deserves sustained and enthusiastic applause."

Ken Adachi, *Toronto Star*

Wayne Grady, editor

THE PENGUIN BOOK OF CANADIAN SHORT STORIES

In this collection of Canadian short stories the very best Canadian writing is sampled. This vast range of stories offers something for every taste and colourfully reflects the rich diversity of one country's literary heritage.

'. . . the short story has developed into Canada's healthiest and most versatile literary genre. Several of our novelists—Morley Callaghan and Hugh Garner, for example—are better known abroad for their short stories than for their novels. And many of our best writers write virtually nothing but short stories: Mavis Gallant, Norman Levine, Alice Munro, W.D. Valgardson, and others.'—*from the preface by Wayne Grady*.

These twenty-eight stories have been carefully selected and introduced to provide both entertaining reading and an insight into the dominant themes and directions of Canadian literature from its beginnings in the early nineteenth century right up to the present day.

Norman Levine

CHAMPAGNE BARN

The twenty-three stories in this collection — a retrospective of Norman Levine's finest work — were written between 1958 and 1978. They beautifully evoke the physical presence of people and the atmosphere of places in a variety of settings in Canada and England.

"Lean, spare, eloquent stories."

Robert Fulford, *Saturday Night*

"Mr Levine is a true artist, who grinds his bones — and anything else he can lay hands on — to make his bread."

Bernard Levin, *The Sunday Times*

"A masterly touch." *Times Literary Supplement*